THE FANTASTIC MUSE
AND
OTHER STORIES

For John and LeeLee, enjoy.
Thanks for your wonderful
hospitality.

Ray

THE FANTASTIC MUSE
AND
OTHER STORIES

A Collection of Short Stories

Ray H. Stieffel, Jr.

iUniverse, Inc.
New York Lincoln Shanghai

The Fantastic Muse and Other Stories

iUniverse books may be ordered through booksellers or by contacting:

iUniverse
2021 Pine Lake Road, Suite 100
Lincoln, NE 68512
www.iuniverse.com
1-800-Authors (1-800-288-4677)

This is a work of fiction. All of the characters, names, incidents, places, organizations, and dialogue in this novel are either the products of the author's imagination or are used fictitiously.

ISBN-13: 978-0-595-41780-3 (pbk)
ISBN-13: 978-0-595-86123-1 (ebk)
ISBN-10: 0-595-41780-9 (pbk)
ISBN-10: 0-595-86123-7 (ebk)

Printed in the United States of America

To my wife, Ann, for
her patience,
understanding and
editing.

Contents

Sand

By necessity, Homer Briggs was a salesman—by ambition he was a writer. This ambition, however, had met consistently with failure as attested to by an abundance of rejection slips. Undaunted, nevertheless, by this graveyard of gladiator manuscripts, fallen in the cruel arena of publishing companies and thumbed down by Nero editors, Homer continued diligently trying to break the print barrier.

Mary was Homer's wife and severest critic. Ruthless, perhaps, would be a better word to describe her faultfinding. Though an avid reader herself, she did little to encourage his literary pursuit.

In fact she used what she read as a club of comparison to pound away at his self-confidence. Her chief criticism was that his work lacked "realism." With this word she hounded him eternally.

Only last night, after quickly browsing his latest effort, she had said, "It's just not realistic, Homer. It sounds too amateurish, too artificial," she whined in disgust. And worse, had followed this with, "Homer, why don't you just give it up? You've got to have something to write about to be a writer.

"Look at London, Hemingway and Michener—those are writers. Where is your Yukon? Your Kilimanjaro? Your Hawaii?"

She had paused briefly, like a fencer who has brought his rapier to the chest of his adversary. Then, relishing the moment before the final thrust, she consummated her attack.

"Face it, Homer, what can you expect when you're nothing but a peddler."

She had never come right out with it before, but his being just an ordinary salesman had always embarrassed her. Before their marriage, she had been a popular socialite. When he proposed, she had accepted, even though she had considered him below her station in life.

She had envisioned herself being married someday to a famous writer who would crown her with social prestige, and she would be the woman behind a famous, successful author. Mary gave an annoyed look at their tiny, inexpensive apartment and frowned at its simplicity, its threadbare rugs and second hand furniture. Then with a gesture of disgust, "This is reality" and left for a night of bridge with the girls.

The sound of the door as it slammed behind her was like an audible exclamation mark. It was the end of a story, he mused bitterly—the story of their life together. Instead of the usual feeling of shame and ineptitude, the sharp, cutting words of his wife had severed something inside him. He felt only a sense of relief—of freedom.

The next day was Saturday. Homer didn't work on Saturdays, at least not at selling. He routinely spent the day at the library writing, reading and re-writing his short stories. This Saturday, as usual, he collected his papers, pencils, thesaurus, dictionary and a thermos of hot coffee, and looking something like a literary safari, rolled out the driveway with Mary fretting about his wasting another day.

Homer didn't come home for lunch or supper, and it was nearly midnight before Mary saw the lights of his car turn unhurriedly into the drive.

From inside, she eyed him suspiciously as he stepped casually from the car, enjoyed a luxurious stretch and began unloading his literary luggage. As he sauntered through the front door she waited for an explanation, but instead received an unconcerned, "Good evening, Mary," and walked past her down the hallway.

She was about to say something sarcastic but sensed an aloofness about him, a detached independence that prompted her to remain silent for the moment.

With arms folded and eyes glaring, she followed him to the bedroom where he unloaded everything, including a reasonably fat manila folder that obviously contained a new manuscript. She watched him sit down and remove his shoes with short grunts of satisfaction. As he started for the bathroom, she could no longer contain herself.

"All right, what have you been up to? Where have you been all this time?" she queried sharply, her voice strident and irritating.

The eyes of the man who paused briefly and looked steadily into her own were not those of the man she had so easily berated the day before. They were sure, confident eyes that were meant to command rather than be commanded.

"I am going to take a shower, Mary. Will you excuse me, please?" The cold pretended politeness of his voice possessed a finality that left her chilled.

The door closed firmly behind him, and soon she heard the wet clatter of the shower. At that moment, a weird sensation overcame her. She had the peculiar feeling that the man behind that door was not her husband.

Still in a quandary, she turned to the bed, and her eyes fell on the manuscript. Intuitively, she felt that it held the answer to the sudden transformation that had occurred in her husband, and with a surreptitious glance at the light shining beneath the closed door, she picked it up and began to read.

The title immediately caught her attention, *"The Girl on the Beach"*. Even the vaguest suggestion of sex was foreign to Homer's plots. She sensed an impending calamity, as yet hazy and without form. Anxiety welled within her, and her thin hand rose defensively to her throat.

The first paragraph stirred mixed emotions of jealousy and anger, finally settling into undefined fear.

"She lay still on the white sands of the beach as the bold sun stared down unabashedly at her body. A mischievous wind slipped deftly beneath the loosened, flimsy cups of the cotton halter, revealing the full, rounded softness of pale, white breasts."

"Homer?" was the singular thought that rose to her mind. And further …

"… lulled by the warmth of a spring sun and caressed by a feathery breeze that shyly explored the marvelously sculptured periphery of her body …"

The shower stopped. He would be out soon, she thought and she began to scan the remainder of the story, her eyes catching words and phrases.

"… her silken thighs … golden hair … the slender length of her legs …"

Beautifully written, she thought grudgingly … so attentive to detail … so disturbing.

"They had just met, yet they were no longer strangers. He lifted her chin with the tip of his finger and for a long moment looked deep into her eyes. His arms held her with a gentleness that belied their strength, and his lips engulfed her own …"

Sensing from a movement in the bathroom that Homer was about to emerge, she quickly returned the manuscript to its folder.

She began to frown, and something not yet quite clear began to trouble her. The change in her husband—his writing … never had he been so masterful. Never had he achieved such realism, such vivid description. Absently, she picked up his shoes to place them in the closet.

A profusion of crystalline white granules rained unexpectedly to the tile floor, crackling and grinding beneath her slippers. The nebulous, undefined anxiety that had evaded her, suddenly congealed. Sand!

Lion

The tropical forest was steaming, and in the hot stagnant air Kris Koenig could feel the sweat running down the small of his back then down his legs and into his brogans.

It was a game of put and take, gulping water by the gallon while the intense heat boiled it out of him in a steady stream. He hated the jungle, he hated the local natives and he had little patience with their naive mentality and superstitions.

They were days deep into a seldom-frequented part of a densely thick area looking for a particular lion. Normally found in the African savanna the lion had apparently strayed. While searching for food and water during a drought he had entered the bordering tropical forest.

Kris was a photojournalist hired by *Animal Worlds* to investigate rumors about an unusual lion. His destination was a little known tribe that was said to have an unusual, cult-like relationship with a huge lion in the area. It was suspected the tribe offered it human sacrifices. Though this had been outlawed by the government, the tribe was so far from civilization and from the law that little could be done to change their customs.

Government trackers had been sent periodically to check on the tribe but some had never returned. Nothing could be proved against the tribe, however. It always appeared to be an accident … and it was always the result of a lion attack. As a precaution, therefore, the government had insisted that Kris be accompanied by two well-armed guards and one of the area's best guides and interpreters. The country prospered from tourism and did not want an incident that might discourage visitors.

Finally, on the seventh day of the safari they found the tribe and the guide explained to Kaiwaki, the tribe's chief, that their intentions were to photograph the lion. The tribe had never seen a camera and when Kris demonstrated with his Polaroid, the natives were astounded and pleased by the white traveler's magic.

All would have gone without incident had it not been for Motako, the tribe's witch doctor. Motako had remained aloof during the photo demonstration and then firmly denounced the safari's plans to intrude on the lion and their tribal life. To Motako, it was demeaning to his people and to the lion that they revered as sacred, and he was convinced that this intrusion by outsiders would bring disaster to the village.

If Kris had made an effort to be more tolerant it might have turned out differently, but instead, he had mocked Motako and his beliefs, causing the old man to lose face among his people. The guards and the guide were quick to warn Kris that he had made a dangerous enemy. The chief, however, pleased by the gift of photographs of himself and his people, overruled Motako and agreed that his people would help Kris to track and photograph the lion.

On the first day of tracking they located the magnificent beast, but Kris, in his impatience, was careless and crowded the huge animal too closely. It had suddenly attacked and killed one of the young blacks from the village.

A deep silence descended on the tribe and the smiles were gone when the body was returned to the camp. Kris was greeted by eyes burning with hatred as he found Motako preparing for the native burial ritual to be held that night. A bier was built in the center of the village and wood had been piled beneath the body of the young boy. He was to be burned and transformed into smoke that would allow him to roam his beautiful forest forever.

That night Motako danced the ritual of death and after a performance of wild gyrations, finally paused and lit the fire. There he remained rigid, his back to Kris, and watched the flames as they consumed the body. Motako raised his head and followed the smoke as it rose and dispersed into the tall trees. A deathly pall fell over the tribe and all that could be heard was the crackling of the flames.

Suddenly, Motako whirled toward Kris where he sat and thrust his voodoo staff inches from the face of the surprised photographer and shook it violently. Then, with unbelievable contortions of his body, he placed the staff between his teeth, flung his head from side to side growling and screaming. His hands appeared to become claws as he raked his chest until blood appeared from the gouged wounds.

There were sharp intakes of breath as the wide eyes of dark faces turned toward Kris. He was shaken for a moment and gripped by fear as the guide, obviously frightened himself, explained that Motako had just placed the "curse of the lion" on him. Even the old chief was seen to cringe from the witch doctor for in this Motako was supreme; no one could challenge his curse. At first Kris had blanched at the words of his guide, then, with a hand on his holster, he forced a false laugh and made a ridiculing gesture toward Motako.

The eyes of Motako fell on Kris and the hatred in the black man's eyes was unbelievably intense. All at once Kris felt as if red-hot ice picks had begun to pierce his chest. He cried out in pain and clutched at his breast. Immediately the guards and the guide moved to stand between Kris and the witch doctor, weapons at the ready. Motako sneered at them contemptuously and slowly turned again to the bier.

As he did so, the pain in Kris' chest subsided but left his face white with fear. Facing the fire, Motako spread his arms high and began a monotonous incantation and was soon joined by the entire tribe including the chief.

Kris rose shakily to his feet and carefully backed away from the circle, his pistol drawn. The guards and the guide joined him and looking over their shoulders, made their way back to their tent and stood guard over what little was left of the night. There was no sleeping for them, for the chanting lament of the natives lasted until dawn, at which time Kris and his party left the village.

The tribesmen watched them in silence as they left. The witch doctor's eyes, burning with hatred, continued to follow them until they disappeared into the thick foliage.

The return to the port was without incident although his black companions, terrified by their experience, continually checked the trail behind them until they had reached the safety of the city. As for Kris, once within the city and civilization, he had dismissed the entire episode and attributed his experience at the fire that night to some type of weird hypnosis and ignorant superstition.

Back in the states, where the photographer lives alone, he is in the process of developing the film. One frame of the lion is an exceptional photo and uncannily realistic. He is sure that it will be very marketable. He leaves the darkroom to call his magazine to lay on space for his story and photographs. It is well into the night when he returns to the darkroom to develop additional copies of the lion to mail to his editor.

There he is stunned. The dark room is a shambles—wrecked! There are deep cuts and scratches on the wall and equipment as though something sharp had torn at it, and on closer inspection he notices what appears to be teeth marks. Ridiculous! Yet, his body shudders as an unnerving premonition numbs his thoughts.

Before his mind can grasp the significance of what has occurred, he eyes fall on the print of the lion—it is blank! What? His mind is still staggering to comprehend as he reaches for the negative. It is also blank. Impossible!

Then from outside the darkroom door he hears a muffled sound. "Who's there?" He stammers. His voice cracks as a rising fear causes his mouth to go dry and his throat to tighten … There is no answer.

At last his scattered thoughts begin to huddle, to congeal. Yet, obstinately, he refuses to accept the sinister suggestion that is invading his mind. Then, to deny it, to dispel such an incredibly stupid idea, he brazenly opens the door.

In the next moment there is a mind-shattering roar and powerful, muscular haunches carry a hairy, sinewy body crashing and snarling into the darkroom. Huge claws rip and tear until the screams of its victim are stilled.

Later that night, Kris's body is discovered by the police as a result of a neighbor who called and reported hearing screams coming from Kris Koenig's home. It is a routine incident as far as the police are concerned, other than the neighbor supposedly hearing screams. There is no evidence of fowl play, no outward signs of violence or marks on the body, and the coroner report indicates death by a massive coronary.

Under a blazing sun, the witch doctor stands staring into the distance, his face a contortion of sinister concentration. Then, there is relief, a relaxation, and the bare trace of a smile. His words are barely audible.

"It is done."

The Vine

It was Saturday morning.

James Crutchfield reluctantly opened his eyes and sleepily began to review his plans for the day. That damn wisteria vine. It was growing all over the fence on the south side of the yard and had seriously begun to attack the beautiful pear and oak trees. Its main root lay somewhere deep in a twisted jungle of growth in the vacant lot adjacent to his property.

The area was terribly overgrown, almost inaccessible, and served as a lair for the well-entrenched vine. The vine was constantly besieging the manicured yard, trying to strangle the life out of his shade trees and defenseless azaleas.

He had been putting off this chore for some time and the vine had taken advantage of his procrastination and established a firm foothold inside his property. Today he would do battle. The thought was exhilarating and roused James' sleep-laden mind and finally enticed him out of bed.

After coffee and breakfast he was ready to engage the enemy. Having donned his combat clothes, which included rugged leather brogans, old khaki pants and a long sleeve khaki shirt, he went to the tool shed to select his weapons for the forthcoming battle.

He gathered together a small limb and vine cutter, a bow saw, machete, rake, and a large, empty vinyl garbage can to haul the vine away. Lastly, he put on his old, floppy khaki hat with its "fifty-mission-crush", which he always wore in the "battle of the backyard." His wife, Joan, bid him farewell as he finally loaded all the tools into an old battle-scarred wheelbarrow and bravely headed for the front lines.

A searing sun was well up into the sky by the time he reached the vine and as he approached it more closely, he was appalled by its size and the extent of its malevolent invasion. It was much thicker than he had imagined. It was intimidating, almost frightening, how fast and aggressively it had grown.

James studied the area. Where to start? There seemed to be fresh tentacles of new growth everywhere. He could almost see them growing, reaching relentlessly toward his home, his family—by God he would put an end to that.

He had decided to locate the heart of the vine and finish it once and for all. He began cutting and hacking his way into a dense area where he suspected the vine had its origin. It was hot sweaty work and the sun beat down mercilessly on the stifling, twisted entanglement. The air was still and pungent with the scent of the cut and dying pieces of the vine. He paused a moment to rest and wipe the salty sweat from his face and burning eyes.

What was that? Was the heat getting to him? Or did one of the tips of the vine actually move on its own? Ridiculous. What a stupid thought.

He had continued to cut when the sensation occurred again. Something was wrong here … He kept cutting and watching … Did it move again? Was it because he had moved? Could it have been the wind? He stopped and looked around him. It was dead still, not a breath of air. He continued to cut but only absently paying attention to what he was doing, his mind preoccupied by something vague and difficult to corner with his thoughts. He sensed a presence …

He had become excessively ensnared in the thick maze when a terrible suspicion gripped him. He stopped, rigid, with only his eyes scanning rapidly left and right.

Then he saw it. There was no doubt this time. In the stillness, he watched as one of the extended ends of the vine nearest his throat, moved of its own accord and then, as though realizing it had been seen, stopped abruptly.

James' mind froze. His eyes became fixed on the increasing entanglement about him. The vine tips were like so many snakes poised to strike. To turn and run was his only thought. Before he could even move, however, his world was transformed into an unbelievable nightmare as ends of the vine began whipping around him.

In sheer terror he screamed but the vine tip near his neck quickly encircled his throat choking his cry. He fought desperately to free himself from its strangling grip but other leathery strands had almost immobilized his arms and legs.

James was panic-stricken. Blinding sweat poured profusely from his body as he struggled to slide his arm through the tightening grip of the vine. Twisting and turning he maneuvered the cutter blades between the vine and his skin and cut the strand that had begun to collapse his throat.

He was beginning to lose consciousness when air burst into his lungs again. He tried to scream but there was no sound. He tried again and this time emitted a loud cry as total terror struck at his heart. Then, several fingers of the vine succeeded in quickly wrapping themselves about his throat again. His chest heaved; he tried to breathe. The world turned darker and darker, then black, and he lost his thoughts.

His throat was burning and raw, and it was difficult to breathe. He opened his eyes and there was his wife, and Mike and Mary Taylor, their next-door neighbors. It was cool and he saw he was in a hospital.

A doctor was talking to his wife, "… an extreme case of heat exhaustion bordering on a heat stroke …"

James knew better. He knew the truth, or was it the truth? Had it been heat exhaustion? Had he really just hallucinated? That was certainly more probable. Perhaps that's all there was to it, he thought, somewhat comforted by that possibility.

James remained silent, however. He would appear mighty foolish describing what he thought had occurred. He waited until he had returned home and was alone, and then went warily again to the vine.

Slowly, he edged closer and noticed the thick pieces of amputated vine that lay fallen on the ground where his wife and neighbors had found him unconscious. When he was only a few feet away, he stopped, closely studying the vine.

Then his mind exploded! Several nubs that were still attached to the main vine began all at once to reach out for him. Stunned, he backed away stumbling then turned and ran for his tool shed.

Grabbing the gasoline can, a bucket and matches, he went back to the vine and approached it cautiously, unable to believe this was realty happening.

He opened the gas can, filled the bucket and threw the gasoline deep into the thick foliage, penetrating to the very heart of the vine. He repeated this quickly several times. He watched, incredulously, as the vine cringed and writhed under the volatile liquid as though aware of his intentions. He lit a match and tossed it into the gasoline. It was like an explosion. Fire mushroomed into huge, billowing flames so hot and intense that he fell back to escape the heat. He listened unbelieving to shrieking, whining cries as the vine shrank and withered, and then turned a deathly black.

When the fire had mainly subsided, only burnt remnants of the vine remained near the ground, exposing its sinister, twisted trunk. Again he poured gasoline on the charred stubble of the trunk and burned it until nothing was left above the ground but ashes.

He knew now that what had happened to him was real, though unexplainable, but also realized this was something he could never mention to another person. No one would ever believe him.

But now, even though the vine was dead, he could not bring himself to continue living in a house that held such horrible memories. Using reasons other than the truth, he convinced his wife they should move and in a very short time they had vacated and new tenants now occupied the building.

It has been several months now, and the incident has been forgotten by all but James. He must forever live alone with this memory. And in the vacant lot, unnoticed by the new tenants, a small, single, bright green beginning of new growth is twisting and emerging from the blackened earth.

The Edge of Eternity

When it first happened it never occurred to me that it was anything unusual. I simply parked my car and was about to enter the Harper Surgical Clinic on a routine call when suddenly, I felt I had just been there, a feeling I often encounter in the course of my work.

My business is medical supplies and carries me at such a hectic pace to scheduled calls on the doctors in my area that sometimes the days and the weeks between seem to grow shorter.

When I approached Harper's Clinic, I knew it had been a week since my last call, yet it seemed only yesterday since I had been there. The feeling was so convincing I actually wondered if I were off schedule. Finally, I brushed the incident aside and finished the remainder of my calls for the day.

After my last call I was driving to my apartment and had stopped by Whitey's newsstand for a paper when it happened again. I had flipped Whitey a quarter and was reaching out for the paper. Hadn't I just been here? I knew I hadn't seen Whitey since yesterday, yet the feeling that it had been only a few hours before persisted.

Then something occurred that was totally strange. For a brief moment Whitey seemed to move away ... but I had been watching him and he was standing perfectly still.

Yet, somehow he seemed distant, and the sounds ... the noises around me seemed to accelerate and grow fainter. Then it was over.

"Anything wrong, Mr. Burton?" Whitey had asked anxiously. "You look sick."

"No, just tired I guess," I answered, "working too hard." I forced a casual laugh that satisfied Whitey and drove on to my apartment half convinced that it was fatigue.

I am usually a sound sleeper, but several times during the night I woke with a start possessed by an unaccountable fear. Why or of what I was afraid I could not imagine, and before my sleep-mottled mind was able to cope, I would slip again into the abyss of my subconscious.

In the morning I was tired and heavy-eyed with traces of this unexplainable fear still lingering. It was no less real but in the light of day I felt more capable and began seriously to consider what had been happening to me.

I thought of the incident with Whitey and the occurrence at Harper's Clinic and wondered if they were somehow related to the restless night I had spent and this peculiar fear that remained.

Still speculating, I got up and walked stiff-legged to the bathroom to shave. Removing my washcloth from its rack, I soaked it in steaming hot water, waited for it to cool a little, and then pressed it against my face to soften the black stubble that had grown there since the morning before. Its warmth was stimulating and a feeling of well-being diluted the anxiety that had begun to seep into my mind.

I held the cloth to my face and closed my eyes. It was a moment's sanctuary. Then, the warmth gone, the blood resumed its normal flow and the softened beard awaited the blade. I returned the cloth to its rack, opened the medicine cabinet and reached for my shaving brush.

Suddenly, my arm grew long and the brush moved away. It didn't actually move, just all at once it was farther away. The water was still running but it sounded faster and quieter—distant.

My movements also speeded up. I looked down. The hand bowl was far below me and I sensed I was going to fall. I dropped the brush and grabbed the basin with both hands to steady myself. I closed my eyes and waited. It must pass. It was as though my world and some alien world had brushed in passing and for a moment I existed in both, not at all sure in which I was to remain. Then all was normal again. It had gone and I felt cold sweat on my face.

The receptionist recognized me as I approached the desk. "Good morning, Mr. Burton, you're early this week, aren't you?" she queried.

"Yes, I am. Got something I believe the doctor will be interested in," I replied, realizing there was more truth to my answer than was apparent. "How are you today, Mrs. Dodd?"

"Just fine, thank you. Have a seat and I'll let the doctor know you're here." She disappeared down the hallway. What was happening could no longer be ignored. There was no panic but I knew I needed help. I had never experienced anything like this in my life. I tried to think about it.

These incidents seemed to occur when I repeated certain routine acts, yet the interval between seemed to be growing shorter. I must be nuts even to consider such a preposterous thought.

Wednesday-to-Wednesday was a fixed interval, from midday of one day to midday of the next was twenty-four hours, yet I could not help but feel that the week itself had somehow really been shorter, or the day had been less than twenty-four hours. What a ridiculous thought.

The hands of the clock still turned, there were still sixty seconds to the minute, sixty minutes to the hour, but somehow all of these increments seemed to have grown shorter, in unison: the minute, the hour, the day—they all seemed shorter.

It was madness, I knew, to think this, and I vacillated between totally discarding the idea and plunging again into the mystery to find an answer to what I was experiencing. That such a thing could happen was so impossible I had concluded that it must be some type of recurring hallucination and the strange physical distortions that accompanied them were the symptoms.

I knew I needed help but realizing how difficult it would be to explain such a thing to someone else I selected a close friend, Dr. Frank Tyler. We had attended the university together and had been roommates.

After a short time Mrs. Dodd motioned me to the doctor's office.

"Sorry to keep you waiting, Jim, what's new?" Frank leaned back in the thick-cushioned leather chair and regarded me expectantly, assuming I was about to detail him on a new medical product as I usually did. I hesitated, wondering how to begin.

"Frank," I said finally, "This isn't a routine call. I have a problem, a very unusual problem, and its nature and implications are rather embarrassing to explain. That's why I've come to you."

Frank's eyebrows drew together, concern momentarily replacing his smile. "Jim, your problem is my problem and together I'm sure we can whip it. Fire away," he said, smiling again.

His confidence was reassuring. It was easier to continue. "Frank, at the present time I feel I am in complete control of my faculties; yet, what has happened in the last day or so has convinced me I am experiencing some sort of mental delusion, or, and I'm fully aware how ridiculous this will sound, time for me has somehow accelerated." I kept my voice even and did not allow the tension that had begun to grow within me to evince itself.

I paused to study the effect of my words on Frank—the lifting of one eyebrow and the slight pursing of his lips were barely noticeable.

I went on and related everything that had occurred, including the mad theory that kept luring me to its conjecture like the proverbial moth to the flame.

I found myself avoiding Frank's eyes as I continued, not wanting to be distracted by the expression of incredulity that had begun to gather on his face.

"Frank, it's as if time has jumped the track … like the sudden breaking of the mainspring of a watch and the hands spin at a dizzy speed, no longer restricted to their conventional movement, and increments. And, as I said, when this happens, the appearance and sounds of everything around me are severely altered. Yet the people around me at the times this occurs seem unaware of the phenomenon. This, of course, makes it logical to suspect that it must be only in my mind. My intelligence tells me it cannot be otherwise. But when it happens, it is real." I began to raise my voice and I realized I was losing control.

I paused again to collect myself then looked at Frank. "I just don't know, Frank, I'm not even certain I have intelligently explained what has been happening to me, but that's it." I finished resigned to whatever conclusions and advice Frank would offer.

At the first mention I made of time accelerating Frank had almost laughed, possibly because it is a sensation familiar to most people and joked about by just as many, but realizing I was serious, he had refrained and studied me in the professional manner of one accustomed to being unexpectedly confronted by life's mysteries.

When I had finished, he began carefully. "Jim, I would certainly hesitate to accept this as actually being some freakish acceleration of time, particularly when it appears to be uniquely confined to your experience alone. We must assume, therefore, that in spite of your apparent normalcy, you are the victim of some sort of hallucination."

There it was, I thought. Then it probably was madness—my madness.

"Your mind," Frank continued, "for some reason unknown to us at the moment, and this reason could account for your fear, is deluding you into believing this to be an actuality. I must point out, however, that though it may not be real to me or anyone else, it is, as you said, real to you and that's what's important. Such a sickness, and I use the word intentionally, for it must be recognized as such, can cause mental as well as physical damage if not treated.

"There are many secrets about the mind that remain hidden from us even with the strides we've made in this field." He considered me for a moment.

"Jim, I'm not a psychiatrist and your problem, being a special one, requires special attention. I have a good friend, Dr. Bill Sheffield, who is an excellent psychoanalyst. With your permission, I'd like to make an appointment for you to see him as soon as possible.

The insinuation naturally disturbed me but I had resigned myself to follow whatever advice Frank gave. I agreed.

"Let me call him now and make an immediate appointment," he urged.

"All right," I said, with some misgiving. I listened as Frank called Dr. Sheffield and related the details of our conversation. There were intervals of silence as he listened to the other doctor's remarks. Each nod of acknowledgement was accompanied by a studied glance at me.

"Yes, I agree, the sooner the better." He looked at me across the desk. "I have ten o'clock," he said, looking at his watch. "Yes, until at least two-thirty, I should be finished by then. Your office at three-thirty?" He looked at me for approval. I nodded. "O.K., Bill, three-thirty. I'll have Jim meet me here at three and we'll drive to your office together." He glanced at me again, "Fine. All right, Bill. We'll see you later. 'Bye."

Frank hung up and smiled reassuringly. "Relax, Jim, and trust us. We'll straighten this out. Bill would like me to accompany you to his office. Since I've known you for so long he feels that I would be of value in his analysis. He also suggests that you begin immediately to keep a record or log of these occurrences indicating the time and circumstances of each incident," he added.

My thoughts went back. It had been eight-fifteen when I got up to shave. I could recall having glanced at my watch and I was quite certain I could remember with reasonable accuracy when I had been at Harper's Clinic and Whitey's newsstand.

"We are also going to make an appointment for lab tests at the hospital in the morning. It is not unusual for a chemical imbalance to produce similar symptoms. In the meantime," Frank went on, "go to your apartment and rest until time to meet me here."

Reaching into his desk drawer, he took out two capsules wrapped in a blister pack and handed them to me. "Here, take these when you get home, they'll help you rest."

"Thank you, Frank," I said, and stood up to leave.

"Jim," Frank said, grasping my hand firmly, "don't worry, we'll take care of you. Trust us. See you here at three, O.K.?"

Outside, I walked to my car, my mind still preoccupied by my visit with Frank. I reached out with my key to unlock the car door.

The day was noon-bright, a cloudless sky, yet everything suddenly dimmed and drew away from me. I felt as if I were being drawn into another world. The din of traffic speeded up and the individual noises merged into one distant wail. I blinked in astonishment and tried without success to bring the world about me into proper perspective.

The city was alive with people and cars that had suddenly grown smaller and farther away. It was like looking through the wrong end of binoculars and everything sounded like a record being played too fast.

I pointed the key at the door lock that appeared far beyond my reach, yet before I had extended my arm to its full length the key made contact. Trying to get the key into the slot was difficult. My hand was so distant it seemed to belong to someone else. It was as though everything I did was by remote control.

Then it was over.

I wasn't sure how long the spell had lasted but I was certain it had been of the longest duration yet and the most severe. I unlocked the door, amazed at the ease with which I did so, and got into the car.

For a while I just sat there, my forehead moist with sweat, and stared at the life that moved about me, unaffected and unconcerned. I thought of returning to Frank's office but decided to go home. I needed to be alone, to think. I checked my watch. Ten-fifteen.

Driving home I began to wonder what it was that triggered these sensations. I knew, that it was always something I had done before but each day was filled with myriad repetitious acts. What accounted for its occurring only with certain select acts at certain times? And what did these acts have in common, if anything? I could discern no key or pattern.

This reminded me of Dr. Sheffield's request that I keep a log. Pulling to the curb, I took out my appointment book and jotted down the time and circumstances of each occurrence, beginning at Harper's Clinic:

Wednesday, August 16
1:00 p.m. (approximate)—calling on Harper's Clinic
5:00 p.m. (approximate)—at Whitey's newsstand

Thursday, August 17
8:15 a.m.—shaving
10:15 a.m.—unlocking car at Frank's office

I closed the book and continued to my apartment, still considering the problem. If I could just avoid repetition maybe the sensation would have nothing with which to relate. Without repetition there would be no time interval between similar acts because there would be no similar acts. And without a time interval there could be no phenomenon of the acceleration of these intervals.

Good God, this is stupid. I felt as though my mind were about to explode. In exasperation I slammed both hands to the steering wheel. "I don't believe this is happening to me!" I yelled.

I opened the door to my apartment, took off my coat, loosened my tie and sprawled on the bed. I lay there for some time staring at the light fixture on the ceiling and listening to the noises outside the apartment when all at once the light grew small, the sounds became distant speeding echoes and the room grew dark.

It was happening again. This time I forced myself to remain calm, to observe, intent on trying to analyze what was happening. My eyes whipped from one part of the room to the other looking to see something not affected by the phenomenon. Even my thoughts raced in the same rapid, staccato so characteristic of these happenings.

The spell achieved a certain tempo and there it remained. My hands gripped the sides of the mattress. I seemed to be falling into an ever-darkening chasm. After what seemed an interminable time, it ended. I glanced at the clock; it was eleven fifty-five. My whole body was limp from exhaustion.

I welcomed sleep.

I bolted upright in the bed terrified. My shirt soaked with sweat. A feeling of having just experienced the strongest sensation yet filled my mind and body and a deep fear was gnawing away inside me. But fear of what? It had happened while I slept. I had dreamed something. What? I looked at the clock. One-fifteen.

Noting the time reminded me again of the log. I took the book from my pocket and noticed my hands were trembling as I made two more entries.

Thursday, August 17
11:15 am—lying in bed
1:15 p.m.—in a dream

Then it came to me—what had happened in my dream. The exact events were hazy but the ending was vividly clear. I had ceased to exist! The shapeless fear that had hounded me now began to take form.

It was a premonition. My hands were still shaking as I reached for my cigarettes, lit one, and took a deep drag. I was finding it difficult to concentrate but I forced myself to think about the dream and its connotation.

These spells had always occurred while repeating something routine, or had they? Maybe the acts themselves had nothing to do with it. Then if it wasn't what I was doing maybe it was when I did it. How could there possibly be a repetition in my ceasing to exist?

I struggled to comprehend and felt that something unknown, something almost predatory, was stalking me ... like death itself!

That was an ugly thought. My tongue began to stick to the roof of my mouth and my throat was dry. How could I cease to exist? I wasn't even sick ... or was I? The first seepage of panic began to escape the dam of disciplined calm I had built around my mind.

I got up, my thoughts racing as I went to the kitchen for a cup of coffee and another cigarette. There was still something evading me, something sinister, still lurking.

I took another drag from the cigarette and studied the entries in the log, feeling that it told more than I understood.

Wednesday, August 16
1:00 p.m. (approximate)—calling on Harper's Clinic
5:00 p.m. (approximate)—at Whitey's newsstand

Thursday, August 17
8:15 a.m.—shaving
10:15 a.m.—unlocking car door at Frank's
11:55 a.m.—lying on bed
1:15 a.m.—in a dream

Noting the circumstances under which each event occurred, I could not see anything they had in common. Checking the times of occurrence, however, I saw for the first time what seemed to be a pattern. I struggled to control my thoughts, to analyze.

From the time at Harper's Clinic to that at Whitey's newsstand had been approximately four hours, but from Whitey"s to shaving the next morning had been about fifteen hours.

Converting to minutes, I subtracted the second entry from the first, suspecting a regular interval between each occurrence. The first interval was two hundred and forty minutes the second was nine hundred and fifteen minutes. This was of little significance. I continued down the other entries.

Then I saw it.

Except during the night, and the first two entries, which had been approximate, the interval between the other incidents (whose time I had recorded with accuracy) had decreased by twenty minutes.

But was the night an exception? I recalled something had caused me to awaken during that night.

I rapidly projected the ominous schedule using the twenty-minute interval. It was then that I realized what had caused the disrupted night, the fearful awakenings. I also corrected the approximate times of the first two entries: Harper's Clinic would have been one-fifteen p.m. instead of one p.m. and White's would have been five-fifteen p.m. instead of five p.m. and while I slept, the occurrences would have happened at eight-fifty-five p.m., twelve-fifteen a.m., three-fifteen a.m. and five-fifty-five am. I looked at the revised log:

Wednesday, August 16th
1:15 p.m.—Calling on Harper's Clinic
5:15 p.m.—at Whitey's Newsstand (240 minutes later)
8:55 p.m.—while asleep (220 minutes later)

Thursday, August 17th
12:15 a.m.—while asleep (200 minutes later)
3:15 a.m.—while asleep (180 minutes later)
5:55 a.m.—while asleep (160 minutes later)
8:15 a.m.—shaving (140 minutes later)
10:15 a.m.—unlocking car (120 minutes later)
11:55 a.m.—lying in bed (100 minutes later)
1:15 p.m.—in a dream (80 minutes later)

I was stunned. My mind reeled at what I saw. In less than ten minutes, at two forty-five p.m. it would happen again. I projected the pattern to its conclusion:

In 60 minutes—2:55 p.m.
In 40 minutes—3:15 p.m.
In 20 minutes—3:35 p.m.
0 minutes

If the pattern held, which it had every indication of doing, there would be more occurrences and at three thirty-five p.m. the interval between would no longer exist! It would be zero!

It was a countdown. My mind recoiled and refused to accept the sinister implication.

"This is crazy!" I cried aloud, "This just can't be happening." But it was—it was real and it was happening to me! Total complete panic swept over me. Frank. I had to talk to Frank. I ran and stumbled through the apartment to the phone.

My hand had just gripped the receiver when it suddenly moved away. Yet I still held it firmly. The sound of the dial tone was barely audible and the numbers grew almost too small to read—the whole room seemed to be fading into darkness. The phone grew small and far away and the beeping sound of the numbers as I pushed them seemed to be fading.

"We're sorry, but the number you have dialed is no longer in service or has been disconnected. Please try again."

"We're sorry, but the number you have dialed is …"

I slammed the receiver down, my mind a whir of diminished sounds and the room became smaller and darker.

"Please! Please!" I pleaded with the inanimate dial, my voice breaking. "Please! Please be right!"

Carefully, through the dim distance, I tried to slow down my hand, to slow down the numbers.

"Dr. Tyler's office, may I help you?" It was a strange voice, not Mrs. Dodd's, a temporary receptionist probably, and at that moment the room returned to normal.

I gaped about me, a swallow caught halfway down my throat. I couldn't talk.

"Hello? Dr. Tyler's office," the voice repeated questioningly. "Yes. Yes I'm here." I was finally able to answer, afraid she might hang up. "Let me speak to Frank, please. Please hurry. It's urgent." I stammered impatiently.

"I'm sorry, but the doctor is with a patient right now. If you will leave your name and number I'll have him return your call", she answered with unconcerned politeness.

Something suddenly snapped.

"My God, lady! I'm Jim Burton! I think I'm going to die!" I screamed. "Let me speak to Frank, for God's sake!"

For a moment there was silence and then Frank's calm, reassuring voice: "Jim, this is Frank, what's the matter?"

Struggling to control my voice, I explained quickly what had taken place since I had left his office, including the log entries. "Frank, I want to see Dr. Sheffield now. Before the time on the log runs out. Something is going to happen, Frank. I'm going to die!" I yelled.

"Frank, you still think this is all in my mind but I know better now. Do you hear me, Frank? I tell you I know. It's right here in the log. You've got to help me before it's too late. For God's sake, please!" I was shouting hysterically now.

"All right, Jim, all right, but you've got to get hold of yourself. I'm sure there's a reasonable explanation for what has happened, even to include those strange calculations you deciphered from your log.

"Jim, you wait there and I'll pick you up as soon as I've finished with this patient and we"ll drive ..." Frank was saying soothingly, patronizingly.

My mind exploded. "Wait hell!" I yelled and smashed the receiver down. I looked quickly at my watch—two-thirty.

I stumbled through the apartment, numbed by fright. The car keys—where in the hell did I put them.

I tore from room to room—table, chair, chest-of-drawers, back to the kitchen—stove, refrigerator—my coat pocket.

I raced back to the bedroom knocking the lamp and night table over—to hell with them. I jammed my hand inside my coat pocket. Thank God.

I burst through the door into the bright sunlight and not bothering to close it behind me, half walked and half ran toward my car.

Then, it came again.

I stopped abruptly in the driveway, about twenty feet from my car, my body weaving to keep its balance in a suddenly distorted and darkened world.

Step by step I began slowly to inch the remaining distance, a distance that appeared to be a full city block, and the pavement seemed far below me. The thought of falling paralyzed me. Slowly, I continued to tightrope my way toward the car. The whole neighborhood was dwarfed and hummed faintly in deep shadows.

"No! Please! No!" I begged. "Somebody help me! ·Please! Somebody! Stop it! Stop it!" I was screaming, half in anger, half in fear.

"Well, for crying out loud, Ruthie, come shee this, would you? Jim Burton crocked plumb out of his mind. And he told us he never touched the shtuff—too goddam good to drink with me, is he?"

Dick Kirkley had been drinking heavily and staggered to the door and out into the driveway.

My God. Not now. I thought, as he weaved down the drive toward me. I struggled to reach my car.

"Hey, ole buddy, thought you never touched the shtuff. Know what I think? I think you're a goddammed hypocrite that thinks he's better than everyone else, that's what I think. You ain't nothin' but a dammed lush.

"Whatsamatta, Ruthie and I ain't good enough for you to drink with?"

I reached the car just as Dick pushed his way between the door and me, spilling his drink down the front of his shirt. "Dick, stop it, you're drunk. I've got to go."

"*I'm* drunk? You're the one that's drunk and you ain't goin' no place until you apologize to Ruth and me for being so goddammed shtuck up, do you hear?"

I panicked. With a rough shove I pushed him away and opened the car door to get in.

"What the hell!" he shouted, and tried to wrestle me away from the car.

A blind rage overcame me. I spun around and swung wildly. My fist landed squarely in Dick's face sending him sprawling to the pavement. Blood gushed from his nose and mouth and I heard Ruth Kirkley scream.

I turned back to the car and rushed to get in but Dick, now transformed into a howling, bloody, vengeful fury, lunged at me from the ground.

"You dirty, lousy bastard! I'm going to knock your goddammed brains out for that, you cruddy ..."

My mind was being torn apart and a bloody-faced man was coming at me with curses and blows.

"I'll teach you, you son-of-a-bitch!" he howled and swung a long, wide roundhouse that missed, causing him to lose his balance and fall at my feet.

I was frantic to be free. Savagely, I kicked wildly with all the power of my right leg and my foot crashed into his face. There was a sound of cracking bone and cartilage as he rolled back on his heels and sagged into a grotesque, silent heap on the lawn.

"Oh my God! You've killed him! Help! Help somebody!" Ruth was screaming.

I ignored her cries and the outraged shouts of some people who had crowded about the driveway from other apartments.

"Call the police!" somebody yelled.

"Grab 'im. Don't let him get away!"

Before they could stop me I got in the car, started the motor and raced out the driveway and onto the street, hitting several men who were trying to stop me. Their own cries were added to those of Ruth Kirkley.

The world was a blur of cars flashing by, screaming people and blaring horns. Then the sounds all at once grew strangely muffled and an unnatural darkness fell across the city ... I was driving through a strangely distorted dream.

Then the world snapped back. I raced through the heavy traffic toward Frank's office, running stop signs and red lights and narrowly missing pedestrians and cars.

Failing to stop at one red light, I collided with another car causing considerable damage. I ignored the other car.

I looked at my watch. Three thirty-two. I had only three minutes to zero!

Seeing my motor was still running and the car still operable, I sped away leaving the other driver cursing and shaking his fist.

I drove wildly. I heard myself crying, screaming—and I felt the edge of eternity.

The collision had been witnessed by two patrolmen who had pulled to the curb to investigate. Both officers had already stepped from their patrol car and were approaching when to their amazement, in broad daylight, one of the drivers had raced away, slamming his hand to the horn and holding it there. The officers had followed in hot pursuit.

Jim raced through the city traffic, the speed of his car and the steady, blaring urgency of his horn caused people along the crowded street to stop and stare. The siren of the police car wailed close behind, the two patrolmen never losing sight of their fugitive.

Frank had tried to call Jim at his apartment and became concerned when there was no answer. Immediately, he called Bill Sheffield.

Both men agreed that he should be hospitalized. Bill said he would be right over and together they would pick up Jim and have him admitted.

The two doctors had just left for Jim's apartment when they encountered what appeared to be an accident at an intersection a block away from Frank's office. Traffic had been halted and was now hopelessly snarled. Frank stepped out and peered impatiently over the tops of the cars.

At the busy intersection, with police and onlookers crowded about it, the doctor recognized Jim's car but could see no sign of Jim. He turned to Bill.

"Come on," he said, "We've got trouble. That's Jim's car up there."

Both doctors got out and moved quickly on foot to Jim's car.

Frank approached the officer who appeared to be in charge, explaining that he was a doctor and that he believed the driver of the car to be a patient of his in need of medical attention.

Still not seeing Jim, Frank described him to the officer, thinking that perhaps he had been injured and taken to the hospital.

"Yeah, that's the guy, all right!" the officer bellowed. "When I get him behind bars you'll be welcome to him. But right now the problem is to find your Houdini friend."

"What do you mean?" Frank asked.

"Well, we were following less than half a block behind this guy, chasing him after he left the scene of an accident. We never took our eyes off him. Suddenly, we saw his car slow down at this intersection, veer to the right and smash head-on into that utility pole." He gestured toward the car and the pole sunken into its crushed front end.

"Our eyes never left the car, I'm telling you," he continued perplexed. "We pulled alongside and immediately jumped out to arrest the guy and poof—no one was inside. There was nothing, I tell you, absolutely nothing.

"I saw everything just as clear as I see you now, yet that man virtually disappeared in the blink of an eye. There was no possible way for the guy to get out of that car without us seeing him."

The officer paused a moment to bark orders at the other patrolman." Joe, get that traffic moving the hell out of here.

"What's more," turning again to Frank, "several witnesses have conflicting stories about what happened. Some maintain that a man fitting your description and the one I saw at the other accident, was driving this car as it approached the intersection, yet others insist that at the time the car struck the pole on the far side of the intersection there was no one at the wheel. Now figure that out." he said, almost hopefully.

"I don't know what in the hell to believe," he stammered, beginning to look a little shaken.

The doctor paled. "Neither do I, officer—neither do I."

Back to the Cave

The tall, lanky form of Matt Turner sits quietly behind his desk staring out the window. Before him is a typewriter and a fresh pack of paper. For some time he remains motionless, as in a trance; then slowly his head lowers and his eyes become fixed on the instrument before him. With an air of resignation his hands move with a strange heaviness to insert a blank sheet into the machine, and robot-like, his fingers feel their way to the silent round disks. There is something stoic about his countenance, of deep resolution, as he begins to methodically thump the keys. My name is Matterson Turner. What I am about to relate is true, though incredible.

It was the seventh of June, 1944, and I was aboard the USS Clarion en route to Europe. I was one of several war correspondents on board. Our ship was one of many in a large convoy and so far the voyage had been without incident. On the night of the seventh, however, as I lay dozing in my cabin, we were struck broadside by two torpedoes—the explosions only seconds apart.

I awoke with a start at the first explosion, leaped panic-stricken from my bunk and started for the door while the loud blaring of the ship's alarm filled the room.

As the second torpedo struck, the ship jerked violently and the lights went out followed by total impenetrable darkness. The lurch of the ship caused me to stumble, slamming my head against the steel bulkhead. My mind reeled incoherently and the alarm stopped. The air was filled with the screeching and moaning of the ship's structure as she listed heavily and began to sink. The sound of rushing water was everywhere.

Suddenly, with a great gush, the room filled with seawater. I struggled to keep my head above the surface, while the odd angle of the ship so confused me that in the dark I could not distinguish floor from ceiling. For a moment I thought my ears would burst, then, with a tremendous jolt, that rocked the entire vessel, the crazy swirling and splashing stopped and it was quiet.

A continuous, throbbing pain pounded at my ears as I tread water and tried to collect my thoughts. I should be dead now. The ship could not have gone to the bottom or my body would have been crushed. My eyes burned in vain to penetrate the absolute darkness as I moved blindly through the floating objects that cluttered the surface. Such total darkness I had never experienced.

The realization of my predicament suddenly gripped me and I screamed for help but in response heard only my own labored breathing and the soft gurgling of seawater. Moving about I found the cabin had taken the shape of something like a pyramid with a small pocket of air trapped at the apex of one corner. I found a pipe that I recalled led to a radiator situated opposite the door. A rough guess placed the door about four feet under water almost directly beneath me.

Breathing was becoming increasingly more difficult and I was beginning to feel drowsy. I decided to try for the door and the surface of the ocean. Perhaps there were lifeboats about. Releasing my hold on the pipe I slid into the black soundless world below.

On my second dive I located the door and after a struggle, managed to open it. At the same time, however, I became nauseated and felt as though my lungs were going to burst. I struggled for the surface, gasping and swallowing salt water. I groped for the pipe and hung there choking convulsively.

I was beaten. I hardly had the strength to reach the door now. I must have been delirious anyway to think I could ever find my way through the inky blackness of the ship and to the surface of the sea that was God knows how far above me. I would surely die from the bends or drown in such an attempt. Yet here it would be a slow death, suffocated in the poison of my own breath.

My grip on the pipe began to weaken and I was on the verge of despair when I remembered something I had learned as a youngster in the scouts. Slipping back into the water I removed my fatigue trousers, buttoned them and tied a knot in the bottom of each leg. Taking a deep breath I went under and blew air into the open end. Repeating this action the legs gradually filled like large balloons and with a final effort I threw myself between them.

Maybe I lost consciousness or just gave way to sleep in my exhaustion, I don't know, or for how long. I had lost track of time. I was very weak now and knew that the depleting air supply was a major cause. It wouldn't be long I thought, and I began to accept the inevitable.

I thought about God and the wrong I had done during my life. I thought of war and how foolish man was to be led into such tragic affairs. What would it all mean to him when he reached death's door? Life seemed unreal at this moment, a vague remembrance of things trivial and shallow. What lay beyond that door was all that mattered now, all that should have ever mattered. But man is imperfect and faces reality only when he must, only when there is nothing else he can do. When there is no place else to go he comes to the door and wonders and looks upon it as a stranger though he has known it all his life. Death was an unexpected guest, and as she peered into the corners of my soul, I was frightened.

Several times I lapsed into unconsciousness, each time expecting eternity to follow when suddenly I realized something had changed … My God, there was light! It wasn't bright but it was there. I could see the walls and shadows; it was a green flickering light and appeared to come from the water itself. Just at that moment it grew brighter and the shadows moved. Moved?

Then, right before me, a silvery glistening object surfaced filling the compartment with a brilliant, scintillating green. I gaped in disbelief. It was a glass sphere, and inside was the face of the most beautiful woman I had ever seen. I struggled to comprehend what my eyes could not deny, but my thoughts, like frightened mice, scampered elusively out of reach.

At first she had apparently not noticed me, and when our eyes finally met, she was startled. For a moment her beauty had rendered me mute and then I was plunged again into total darkness. She was gone.

"Wait!" I yelled. "Help me!" I listened. Not a sound. I thrashed about the room and found the pipe again. I hung there and heard myself whimpering inarticulate sounds of fear and anger.

I was exhausted and couldn't catch my breath. I tried to think but my mind would not listen. My thoughts ran into each other and I lost my fatigue pants. My hands were weak and wanted to sleep; my mind was letting go and my heart was trying to get out. I lost the pipe and found it again. I slept and the pipe ran away again … and it was funny, it was all so hilariously funny … because I laughed. I cried out and frightened the pipe away again.

The green sun was blinding me. The soft small hands helped and it smelled sweet … it was wonderful, and my lungs awoke. I could see again and my heart stopped fighting.

At first I thought my vision was blurred. Then I realized I was looking through a similar glass sphere and breathing more easily. And she was there again, and so beautiful.

My smile of gratitude was quietly accepted by my visitor. I realized now why she had left. I tried to speak but this proved futile from within the sphere. She smiled at my failure, a smile as warm as the summer sun. She was the perfection of beauty and my heart skipped a beat as I realized that she was wearing nothing but the sphere. Yet, there was no indication of embarrassment; it appeared to be her natural way, and I smiled to myself. What could be more natural?

In a glance I studied the sphere and what appeared to be air tanks, yet something about the material and workmanship appeared strange, strange in that it seemed flawless, but to be more accurate, they were of a quality far superior and more advanced than anything I had ever seen before, almost alien.

She smiled at the attention I was giving the equipment and her eyes shifted to what appeared to be some type of flashlight strapped to her wrist. It was the source of the brilliant green light.

Abruptly, as though she had been late in making the decision, she motioned for me to follow and submerged. The water was clear and the light shone brightly on the open door of the cabin as we passed through and started up the companionway to the main deck. The glass sphere and its tanks provided the weight needed to overcome buoyancy and maneuvering offered no problem.

I was fully conscious now but mystified by what was happening. Who was this girl? Where did she come from? And where was she taking me? I wanted to think about these things. I knew there had to be an explanation but things were moving too fast. Her nudity gave rise to uninvited thoughts that had no place in my mind at this time. Yet ...

Reaching the main deck the eerie beams of filtered sunlight revealed a fantastic world. I was like a child not knowing what to look at first. The heavenly creature that swam before me defied description, while around us was the most spectacular panorama I have ever seen. At that moment she glanced back at me, smiled and pointed toward the surface of the sea and my world.

The ship lay balanced at an angle on the craggy ridge of a huge rock mountain. A myriad of fascinating creatures floated and streaked about, some stopping to gape in curiosity while others swam unconcerned within a few feet of me.

I swam to the ship's rail and looked down, marveling at the clearness of the water. I could see hundreds of feet below me where the sea finally turned to a deep impenetrable blue.

As I looked up I approximated the surface to be some seventy feet above me. In my excitement my attention had been momentarily diverted from the girl and when I turned to look for her she was gone.

I quickly scanned the ship but did not see her. Then I saw her swimming away from the ship toward the mountain. Moving to the ship's rail I started to follow her, determined to find out who she was and how this strange meeting had occurred. My heart told me the other reason.

Then I saw it. Blended against the gray of the mountain, the form was vague but unmistakable. It was a huge shark! It must have been twenty feet long and was stalking her from beneath. Instinctively, I yelled a warning but the muffled sound of my voice from within the sphere told me how futile my effort was. I stood in petrified helplessness as the shark drew nearer, then with a frightful burst of speed it closed the remaining distance to the girl.

Things happened so quickly that I was still staring, my mouth agape in wonder, as she continued to the rocky slopes of the mountain. At the last moment she had seen her attacker. Extending the flashlight object in its direction, a narrow, bright red, laser-type beam had cut through the sea like a bullet and struck the huge fish. Instantly, the shark had quivered, writhed convulsively, and sank limply to the depths below. She had reached the mountain now and I watched her disappear into a dark cave beyond a rocky crag.

For a moment I hesitated to follow. The attack of the shark and the effectiveness of the weapon used to kill it left me with a deep respect for both. This was all so unbelievable. I was Matt Turner, correspondent, and somewhere above this ocean a war was going on and I was part of it. It was a strange feeling, like slowly awakening from a dream, when for a moment it is difficult to distinguish fantasy from fact.

I was between two worlds. Less than twenty feet from me was a cork life raft and a coil of line well over a hundred feet in length. I had only to attach it to the raft, allow it to rise, and slowly follow it hand over hand to the surface, and my world.

But the face of the girl haunted me, the desire to see her again, to learn the meaning of her existence under the sea was overpowering. I made my decision.

I had taken no more than a few strokes toward the mountain, when I sensed a movement above me. One glance sent me scrambling back to the ship. Another shark was plummeting toward me.

It was too far to try for the door so I lunged for the raft and made a frenzied effort to bury myself behind it. I panicked when I was unable to pull my head down because of the glass sphere. I struggled wildly to squeeze between the raft and the ship's bulkhead and at the last second slid snugly in.

In the next instant, razor sharp teeth were ripping fiercely at the raft that jerked and shuddered under the attack. Just then the raft lifted with surprising speed, the shark's teeth had cut the tie lines. I clung flattened against the bottom and in a glance, I saw the shark make only a halfhearted attempt to follow, apparently confused by the unexpected turn of events.

The raft rose quickly, my ears began to ring and a terrific pain knotted my stomach. My God, the bends! A warm liquid filled my throat and I couldn't breathe and I began to tear at the object that smothered my head until I was free of it.

I was sick … being tossed about. Rising … falling … It was hot, very hot, and dry, so dry. It was still … very still … and quiet. A warm breeze was blowing across my body … It was dark … so many stars … and I was cold.

Bright, brilliantly bright … and it hurt my eyes. It was hot, and dry and my throat died. Another darkness, and the stars, so many stars, swinging and swaying, back and forth, back and forth … Voices. I moved. It was cool, beautifully cool and my throat lived again … Rocking, rolling, back and forth … always. And I slept, a deep bottomless sleep.

I awoke and recognized the unmistakable rhythm of a ship at sea. When I opened my eyes, they were met by the intense gaze of a stranger in uniform, our uniform.

"We almost gave up on you, son, but it seems like you are a very determined man."

The sound of the spoken word seemed odd and unreal, it had been so long since … Slowly, my mind began to awaken, to think—to remember.

He was still talking, his voice sounded distant and hollow. My body tensed, as vague recollections became vivid memories. Had it really happened? Of course it had. She was too beautiful, and the shark … too real. There was only one way to know. I had to go back. I must go back. But where?

"Where did you find me?" I asked. My voice sounded strange, and hoarse and my throat hurt. The abruptness of my question stopped him in the middle of a sentence. At first he seemed perplexed, and with a smile he answered. "Why, in the ocean, my boy, in the ocean." he laughed, apparently amused by my question.

"Where in the ocean?" I asked in a tone that did not acknowledge his humor and demanded an answer. The smile left his face and he looked disturbed.

"Where?" he repeated my question, apparently concerned by my interest in what could only be answered in degrees of latitude and longitude.

My better judgment told me it would be best not to pursue the issue, and my intuition warned me to be guarded, to be careful what I said, but I could not help myself. I had to know.

"Look, I know we keep records of where ships sink. Why are you avoiding my question? I've got to know this." My voice cracked again with mounting tension. God, suppose they don't know, I thought. "Someone does know, don't they?" I asked, having difficulty controlling my voice.

"Easy, son, you've been through quite an ordeal and sometimes under that kind of stress, the mind can play some pretty fancy tricks."

He was about to add something, but the sudden indication that he knew what had happened startled me. I tried to sit up but for the first time realized I was strapped hand and foot to the bed.

"What the hell is this?" I screamed, tugging at the thick webbed straps.

"Take it easy, son. Easy does it," he said softly. "I know what you're going through and I think I can help, but first let me introduce myself. I'm doctor McKeen. I'm a psychiatrist."

I shot a quick glance at the straps and then back to the doctor. My God, he thinks I'm …

"Now don't go jumping to conclusions. What you've experienced is not that unusual, this has happened to many men in combat, and the condition is only temporary. It's just a matter of realizing that these things do happen, and that you are not the first person to experience such a psychological phenomenon."

I felt sick. Psychological phenomenon?! What was he saying? And how could he know?

"You see," he went on, "while you were unconscious you spoke of a very strange experience, you know, like talking in your sleep, and though it was unusually detailed, you must realize, this is all a result of the subconscious run rampant." He spoke with an assurance that presupposed an enlightened acceptance from me.

It would have been very easy at this point to act as though I understood and how I had fallen victim to a common hallucination. But I knew this had been real and I felt that in denying it I would be rejecting my own integrity, and somehow I would be betraying what I felt for the girl. I knew what I had seen.

It had not been my imagination. It had happened and somebody had to believe me. I had to go back there, regardless of the consequences. I had to go back …

Two small boys are walking along the sidewalk clicking their sticks on the tall black wrought iron fence. As they pass the large gate, the guard grumbles something at them about being quiet.

Through the fence can be seen a large brick building, several stories high, surrounded by extensive, beautifully landscaped grounds. There are many windows and through one stares the eyes of a man. He doesn't see the beauty of the grounds, nor does he hear the laughter of the boys as they scrape their sticks on the fence. He sees only a face, a face known to him alone, and a smile as warm as the summer sun. He takes her hand and together they swim to the crag and into the darkness of the cave beyond.

A Sixth Sense

The wooden swinging doors whipped open with a clatter as Kreider's dusty gaunt form moved into the saloon. His face was shadowed beneath a trail-worn, wide-brimmed hat, worn low across his eyes. He swiftly scanned the smoke-filled room.

The piano player stopped, grabbed his beer, and scurried behind the bar. The festive sounds of merrymaking quickly retreated, as did the dozen or so anxious cowhands, each seeking the nearest available cover.

Standing at the bar, his back to Kreider, Stringer studied his adversary intently in the mirror. He knew that only seconds remained and his mind worked rapidly with the deadly analysis of a professional gunfighter.

The first movement of the door had caught Stringer's eye and from that instant, his mind had excluded all else. It was as if the rest of the world had ceased to exist and Kreider alone filled the remaining vacuum, real and threatening. His whole being converged on this man, isolating him, carefully studying every detail.

In a glance, Stringer had taken the measure of his opponent: his build, stance, mobility and reach. Almost in the same instant that Kreider made his dramatic entrance, Stringer arrived at a factor somewhere between this man's strength and weakness that indicated his overall speed and ability.

Then quickly he studied the man in more detail; the shape and thickness of the gun hand and length of the gun barrel, which told him how much barrel-whip could be expected, or how far the bullet might stray from its intended mark due to the weapon's rifling. This would enable him to determine in which direction to shift his body to avoid a fatal wound. He noted Kreider's stiffened frame. The leg and arm muscles were too tight to respond smoothly when the crucial moment arrived. He paid particular attention to Kreider's wide-brimmed hat worn too low across the eyes for clear vision.

To Stringer it was like reading a book for the second time. He knew the plot by heart. He would turn slowly and face Kreider and their eyes would meet. Then would follow a period which, to the bystander, would appear as inactivity. It is during this time, however, that gunfighters are made or laid in a pine box. There would be an almost imperceptible tightening of the lips; a narrowing of the eyes, relaxing of the gun arm and the fingers of the gun hand would slowly spread in anticipation.

Finally, the weight of the body would shift almost unnoticed to the leg on which the leather holster was strapped and the shoulder on the same side would lower, placing the gun hand closer to the handle of the weapon. This would not go undetected by Stringer, however, for he missed nothing. Then, the eyes of both men would narrow and darken—the last sign before the draw.

The exact moment of the draw could never be predicted by any visible means. Up to a point, two gunfighters could be equal in their ability. It was that nebulous insight, a sixth sense, found in only a few gifted individuals that ultimately made the difference.

Stringer was one who had mastered this second sight. Like fluid marble he stood motionless, every muscle and nerve in his body tuned perfectly for the mysterious communication of that instant.

It was over. He returned his Colt .44 still smoking to its rawhide holster. The doors of the saloon clattered again as he left, the expression on Kreider's face still hidden by the wide-brimmed hat worn too low across his eyes.

2120 Oak Street

I watched the nondescript car ease to the curb and turn off its lights. It attracted my attention because at three o'clock in the morning it was the only sign of life on Oak Street.

After a short time the car door opened noiselessly and a tall shadowy figure slid out, waited a moment, then quietly and surreptitiously closed the door. The dark night shadows of the sprawling, moss-covered oaks concealed his movements as he walked almost invisibly down the sidewalk toward me. I was more than just casually interested in his behavior now.

For a time he and the night were one. Then, as if emerging from the tree itself I made out his form standing against the blackness of the large oak in front of my porch. Who was this man? And why had he stopped here?

These questions had barely formed when, with the sudden quiet agility of a cat, he sprang toward me. Before I could comprehend that this sinister individual actually meant to approach my door, he had bounded up the steps and glided soundlessly through the entrance—the lock long since inoperative. Once inside I could hear his breath come short and heavy as he groped his way through the inky obscurity of the hall. What could he possibly want? I had nothing to offer a thief.

Recovering somewhat from his brazenness, I became indignant and wanted to shout, Who are you? What are you doing here? But I couldn't. I was helpless. Glancing apprehensively over his shoulder, as if sensing someone was watching him, he stealthily descended the steep steps to the cellar, the old wooden steps crying out in timid protest against his presence.

Once in the cellar, he moved to a large closet and removing the wooden shelves, stacked them against each other on the floor in the corner. Reaching inside his coat, he withdrew a folded wad of newspaper, and out of his pockets took a small can of lighter fluid, a folder of matches and a partially consumed pack of cigarettes. Placing these articles on the floor he began tearing the newspaper into strips and stuffing it between the old shelves.

I watched terrified as the full import of his actions became apparent. This just couldn't be. In heaven's name, why? I didn't know this man. Why would he do this to me?

My thoughts raced in confusion like frightened sheep as his hunched shoulders became silhouetted by the flickering yellow glow of a match. The eerie light revealed a sallow, drawn face and exposed momentarily a countenance evil enough to match his deed. He was a bony-faced man, with wide bulging eyes that glistened like milky agates, and the sickly yellow skin of his face sought refuge beneath a splotchy scraggly beard.

Pinched between his lips, the end of a cigarette burned bright red and dimmed in unison with the contracting hollows of his cheeks. With the cigarette dangling from his mouth he picked up the match folder, bent the cover behind the matches, and tore off a small piece near the heads.

I watched in stunned silence as he mounted the lit cigarette between the heads and the cover. Drenching the paper and wood with lighter fluid, he carefully situated the device so when the cigarette burned down it would ignite the match heads which would in turn ignite the fluid, paper and wood.

I had always accepted my inability to move as a natural limitation, but now I bitterly resented this impediment. With unrestrained desire I wished vehemently to avenge myself. This evil person must not go unpunished for his wanton crime, and I must see that he does not. I must! It was then that I experienced a strange sensation. Something warm and wonderful permeated the lifelessness that was me. Quickly he inspected his fire preparations, assuring himself it would work, then visualizing the holocaust to follow, moved rapidly up the steps with a marked disregard for caution.

The splintering snap echoed through the quiet of the empty house like a clap of thunder as the old step collapsed, and the body of a man, his arms uselessly flailing the air, crashed through the old railing and landed on the concrete below with a sickening impact. He lay there motionless.

An ever-increasing glow burst finally into large tongues of flame that greedily devoured the old building. The tormented shrieks of twisting, writhing timber were a cacophony of sound.

I feel no pain. I am grateful that his remains lay smoldering here with mine. Fate was generous. It granted my only wish in the seventy odd years of my existence in this world of stillness. It allowed me one act—revenge. And, such an occurrence is rare indeed, for you see, I *was* 2120 Oak Street.

Affair of Honor

The early morning sun had barely begun its charge of discovering the new day when the castle drawbridge lowered with a resounding impact, its great chains roaring their displeasure at having to relinquish the quiet slumber of the night's repose.

Then, slowly, the huge portcullis yawned forth its first peasants for the day's work. Mounted on mules and dilapidated old wagons, they moved lazily with their primitive tools across the stagnant moat and down the winding mountain road to the rich farmland in the valley below.

Starkenburg was one of two castles that crowned the fringe mountains of the Odenwald and its vast forest bordering the Rhine Valley. The other, called Auerbach, was located only a few miles away along the same ridge.

The two fortresses had been constructed to serve as guardians of the old monastery at Lorsch, a small settlement situated along the trade routes between the Odenwald and the Rhine River.

Each was ruled by a baron who was master of the soldiers and peasants living there. It had been almost ten years since the invading Swedes had been driven back to the north and the soldiers, as well as their masters, had grown restless in their inactivity. As could be expected, such idleness had caused the trivialities of life to be magnified with the passage of these uneventful years.

At Starkenburg was Baron von Eisenmann, an exceedingly ambitious young man in his early thirties, whose personality was characterized by a fanatical desire for power and recognition. His obsession for acclaim so possessed him that such vague intangibles as honor, chivalry and fair play had been buried beneath an avalanche of petty, egotistical desires.

Such noble traits were used by him only as a matter of convenience to perpetrate his own self-esteem. They served only as catalysts in the selfish equations he contrived to accomplish his own ends.

His world was not a large one and already he had scaled high on the wall of success. He had not, however, been able to attain his ultimate goal, for there stood in his way a formidable obstacle in the person of Baron von Friederick of Auerbach.

Baron von Friederick was an elderly gentleman of seventy years and revered by all who knew him—all, that is, except Baron von Eisenmann.

Though his shock of hair had long since grown white, his vitality had been reluctant in abdicating to old age. In the stature of the old man there remained strong evidence of the once sinewy, panther-like resilience that in his younger days had stirred mixed feelings of fear and admiration among those who had opposed him.

Baron von Friederick had grown old gracefully, never for an instant forfeiting an ounce of his noble manhood. He had retired, his record unblemished, as champion of the land, and now, because of his age, was no longer expected to defend the cherished title he had earned. Consequently, regardless of the great men who had risen after him, the unconquered old warrior had become almost legendary and remained the indisputable idol of his countrymen.

The barrier of the "untouchable" which surrounded von Friederick had all but driven Baron von Eisenmann mad. Though the young baron had vanquished all known contenders of his day, he had been robbed of conclusive victory. The old baron held the place of highest honor and was unassailable. For should von Eisenmann challenge the elderly patriarch, the people would cry out against such an unchivalrous act and condemn him as a barbarian without honor. Then, regardless of the outcome, he would lose face and all he had worked for would be lost.

But, should the old man challenge him, the ensuing contest would be accepted in the eyes of all and when he had won, the image of von Friederick would be destroyed and he, Baron von Eisenmann, would be acclaimed as the unquestioned champion.

High up the sheer stone walls of Starkenburg a loud bellowing suddenly rent the tranquil morning. From the chambers of von Eisenmann was heard the howling profanity of a man truly enraged. His servants huddled before him like frightened sheep.

"I don't give a rusted breastplate if your necks are broken, you go again tonight, and tomorrow night and the night after that until your work is done!"

Baron von Eisenmann was in the process of unmercifully admonishing his servants. It had been three days now since he had implemented his conniving plot to aggravate Baron von Friederick into challenging him. Three whole days since he had sent his servants nightly to mix with those of von Friederick in the numerous wine and beer cellars that lay along the cobblestone streets of Lorsch.

His scheme had been one of slander, accusing the old baron of cowardice, and was designed to rile von Friederick into defending his name. His servants had been the instruments of dissemination and most of them still bore black and blue marks resulting from the fiery disagreements in which they had been entangled.

His plan should have brought results by now and though his servants had exhibited their injuries as witness to the sincerity of their efforts, he still stormed about threatening to have their heads. His terrible obsession had so taken hold that his every utterance was one of a growling, snarling lion, lustful for the blood of its prey. "I will have at him!" he screamed, in such a thunderous roar that the servants all but trampled one another in their flight down the spiraling sandstone stairway.

It was mid afternoon and the August sun lay thick and hot upon the land surrounding Starkenburg, and little sign of life could be seen about the castle as its inhabitants sought refuge from the stifling heat. The Odenwald nudged close to the old fortress and with a noble gesture the tall stately spruce trees offered their shade.

Then, incongruous with the sluggish afternoon, the lazy spell was broken by the vibrant sound of hoof beats as they pounded their way out of the forest, across the small clearing and onto the drawbridge. The hollow drumming of the horse's hooves on the wooden planking echoed throughout the castle, causing a half dozen sentinels to peer in unison over the ramparts.

The knight on the bridge wore the colors of Auerbach and in his hand he brandished a gleaming broadsword on which was impaled a mailed glove with a small scroll attached.

For a brief moment he scrutinized the befuddled faces of the sentinels. Assuring himself that his presence had been noted, he then dug his spurs into the ribs of his steed. The magnificent animal reared high into the air voicing its protest with an ear-splitting neigh and in the same instant the knight shouted, "Baron von Eisenmann!"

Bringing the horse's fore hooves back to the bridge with a loud report, his right arm shot downward, imbedding the sword deep into the back of the bridge. Then with a flourish of his colors the knight whirled toward the forest and in a few seconds powerful haunches had carried him from sight.

Almost immediately the portcullis raised and after considerable difficulty one of the soldiers succeeded in removing the sword and hastened to deliver it to his master. Von Eisenmann had been the first to note the knight's approach and had jubilantly observed the entire spectacle. "The old fool bit. He bit, I tell you. Now, he is mine! My quill! Parchment! Make ready the knight errant!" It was only a matter of minutes before a knight was making his way speedily across the ridge toward Auerbach, broadsword in hand to accept the challenge.

From a window high in one of the twin towers of Auerbach, steel gray eyes looked out across the motionless sea of green. For a long moment they remained fixed on the castle in the distance, then returned to the room.

Contrary to what von Eisenmann had thought, Baron von Friederick had been quick to note the scandalous rumors that had begun to blacken his name and in spite of the advice of his closest friends, who feared that age may have worn dull the once razor sharp senses of their old comrade, the baron had decided to defend his honor.

For ten days von Friederick subjected himself to the most rigorous training, pitting his wiles against the most skilled adversaries in his castle, and when he believed himself ready, dispatched his knight to Starkenburg to deliver his challenge.

Word of the forthcoming encounter rushed like a flash flood across the countryside and when the day of the great contest finally arrived the entire population had crowded about a shaded area in the monastery courtyard, the site mutually agreed on by both men. As the chapel bell tolled the first hour of the afternoon, both barons had arrived with a small contingent of knights, who according to tradition, would serve as witnesses to a fair match.

The two men dismounted and approached an old monk seated behind a rough-hewn oak table. Before him lay an ornate, beautifully carved wooden box. With grave ceremony the elderly abbot began the accustomed explanation of the rules and a hushed silence fell across the onlookers.

Both men listened with grim solemnity until the monk had finished. Satisfying himself that there were no questions, he leaned forward and opened the wooden box. The sight of its contents caused the blood of both men to run hot with anticipation.

First Baron von Friederick and then Baron von Eisenmann were seen to reach forward and the box was emptied. Facing one another in cold deliberation, they waited for the old monk's signal and the struggle began.

Unable to control his eager confidence von Eisenmann moved toward von Friederick in an almost reckless attack and beads of sweat were seen quickly gathering above the drawn brows of the old man.

For the first hour Eisenmann carried the battle to the older baron who had been forced to remain on the defensive due to the sheer weight of the younger man's aggressiveness. Von Eisenmann tested his adversary with a bold, relentless attack designed to break down his opponent's defense.

By the end of the second hour the old peer had been driven into a corner but in spite of this he was still managing to successfully thwart Eisenmann's attack.

On several occasions von Eisenmann changed tactics radically in an effort to confuse the old man but to no avail. The once cocky expression of the young baron began to settle into worried anxiety for he had used every trick he knew and was beginning to sense an ominous futility. Then he saw it. Von Eisenmann blinked his eyes in disbelief. The right flank of the old man was exposed at one point and it seemed fatigue had rendered him unaware.

Gradually, ever so cautiously, von Eisenmann maneuvered himself into a position that would assure him absolute victory when he struck, being extremely careful not to disclose his intention …

"Now!" cried von Eisenmann, dropping all caution in his move.

"Aha!" shouted the old baron in gleeful triumph—von Eisenmann paled, his body sagged—he had seen the trap too late.

With deft certainty the old man had acted with the experience of a master. Savoring his words with delightful relish, the old warrior broke the embarrassing silence:

"Baron von Eisenmann, you young rascal, you are beaten. Checkmate!"

A Lesson in Sales Resistance

It was lunch break and I was munching a cold roast beef sandwich and gulping a soda with my buddy, Fred. Suddenly, his mouth full of food, he turned and blurted out to me, "Say, Bill, guess what happened to me yesterday?" and managed to tongue a piece of tomato back into the corner of his mouth. "You know Pete Smith … works with the crane over in yard 'B'? Well, he comes up to me and asks how would I like to make a quick fifteen bucks."

"What was the catch.?" I asked Fred.

"Believe it or not, Bill, there wasn't any. All he wanted me to do was to let some character demonstrate his company's vacuum cleaner."

"What? You're putting me on." I said.

"No, I mean it, Bill. This is legit. This guy will pay fifteen dollars just to let him demonstrate his vacuum cleaner to you and your wife. What's more, I get another ten dollars if you let him."

"Now I know you're crazy. Nobody is going to pay twenty-five dollars just to demonstrate a vacuum cleaner. What do you have to sign?"

"Nothin', I promise. Look, I'm not pulling your leg. I already got the demonstration, the fifteen dollars and Pete got his ten."

"And nobody bought anything?"

"I didn't say that. Pete bought one because he needed it, but the one we have is still in good condition, so we didn't.

"And this guy just upped and paid fifteen dollars for showing you how it works?"

"That's right."

"And you didn't have to sign anything, right?"

"That's right."

"Well, I'll be darn. That's hard to believe. How long did it take?"

"About twenty minutes. That figures at about forty-five dollars an hour, Bill. Pretty good pay if you could do it regular. How about it, pal? That'd be ten bucks for Janet and me and fifteen for you and Marge and another ten if you could get a friend to agree to a demonstration also."

"Yeah, that's right, isn't it" I replied, already planning what I could spend the money on.

"Bill, you know good 'n well that if that salesman comes here with a new vacuum cleaner you'll buy it," said Marge, "especially since our old one is in such poor shape. You know perfectly well we can't afford it now and you also know you haven't the least bit of sales resistance. You always end up buying. I just don't trust you, Bill," was Marge's candid rebuttal.

"Now look, Marge, if it was a new gun or rod and reel or color TV, you might have something to worry about, but a vacuum cleaner? Come on, all I'm interested in is that fifteen dollars. For gosh sake all we have to do is let that joker salesman clean our living room carpet for twenty minutes and we've picked up fifteen dollars, and if I explain this to Mike and Betty or Jake and Eileen we can get another ten dollars plus throwing money their way. What can we lose?

"Well, all right." said Marge reluctantly, "But I want you to promise me you will say nothing, absolutely nothing while that salesman is in the house"

"Agreed," I said, "all I'll do is thank the guy for the fifteen dollars when he packs up his vacuum to leave, O.K.?"

We had just finished cleaning up from dinner and I had taken my newspaper into the living room to wait for the salesman and his fifteen dollars when there was a knock at the door.

"Good evening, I'm John Freeman with the Versatile Vacuum Company and I was told by Mr. Fred Taylor that you would be expecting me."

Marge rushed to the door and edged between us, forcing the salesman to address her rather than me. Remembering my agreement with Marge, I backed off and made myself comfortable on the sofa, patiently ready to endure the sales pitch before collecting.

After a few opening remarks proclaiming the reputation of his company and the superiority of their product, he explained why it was not a highly advertised vacuum cleaner.

"Why spend thousands of dollars on TV, radio and newspapers, when people would never believe what we told them unless they saw it for themselves.

That's why we rely on personal demonstrations and give the money to you instead."

He sounded very convincing, and it really did make sense. I was glad he was talking to Marge and not to me.

"First, let me demonstrate the Versatile Vacuum's extraordinary sweeping capability."

My eyes widened as I saw him open a small metal box and begin to scatter assorted items all over our carpet, including some small nails, rubber washers, an assortment of buttons, string and plain old dirt. With a flourish of confidence the salesman plugged in the cord, flipped a switch and the machine whirred quickly to a powerful drone.

Like some ravenous animal it proceeded with deft efficiency to gulp each and every object into its bloated stomach. The ease with which it removed the veritable junk yard was impressive and I was about to remark how impressed I was but a glance at Marge and her poker face reminded me of my promise to remain silent. In an attempt to imitate her I folded my arms and stared impassively at the salesman who had turned to me for what he considered much deserved praise.

My expression, bland and unimpressed, momentarily unnerved him. Then, with the resilience characteristic of a good salesman, he continued.

In the following sequence and with equally impressive results, the machine displayed a startling versatility: floor scrubbing, waxing and polishing, Venetian blind cleaning and deodorizing.

"… and all for just $350.00," he was saying as he brought his presentation to a close.

Though initially interested I had become more or less indifferent as the demonstration went on, smugly satisfied with myself for having negotiated such an easy fifteen dollars and for having stuck to my agreement with Marge. I noticed that Marge's deadpan expression throughout had noticeably perplexed the salesman in his feverish attempts to interest her. Marge was tough, and she was right, of course. I was and always had been an easy mark for a salesman. Would you just look at her, I thought to myself, what a lesson in sales resistance.

Anxious to collect my fifteen dollars and be rid of Mr. Freeman, I stood up suggesting that the demonstration was over and that I had seen enough and was not interested.

It happened so quickly I was still standing in stunned silence after the door closed.

"How much are the payments?" They were the only words Marge had uttered.

"$ 13.90 a month," he answered quickly.

"We'll take it," she said.

Waterspout

(Based on a True Story)

To those who are not familiar with the sport of sailing, the sight of a slow moving sailboat off shore might cause them to surmise—what a bore. There are times, of course, when the wind is light, that sailing is slow but this is only one face of the sport, and frankly, on occasion I enjoy a soft gentle breeze to lull me into a lazy, sleepy mood. I find it a healing experience—an escape from the frenzy of the workaday world. But as I said, this is just one face of the sport.

It depends on whether you are racing or cruising. Cruising is done leisurely, while racing can be frenetic. For the most part, however, it is Mother Nature that decides what a particular outing will be like, whether calm or traumatic. I'm sure we have all heard the expression, "the many faces of the sea." Well, for each face the sea has a matching personality. The following is a true story of Mother Nature in one of her poorer moods.

I was skippering a twenty-foot centerboard sloop with low freeboard. I had two passengers: Alice Dupaquier, my wife's sixty-nine year old aunt—very much into life, and never letting age stand in the way of an adventure. Sailing was not new to her. She and her brothers had grown up during the days of "iron men and wooden ships" along the Mississippi Gulf Coast.

My other passenger was Nannette Stroh, a twenty-two year old cousin of my wife, who was looking forward to the adventure. The evening before, they had both been to our home for dinner and had remarked that they had not yet been for a sail on my boat, and in the spirit of the evening I invited them for a sail the next day.

By the time Aunt Alice and Nannette arrived at the harbor, I had already rigged the Gulf Coaster and raised the sails. I was watching some rather squally

looking weather building up to the south and frankly, had I not been committed to take them for a sail, I don't believe I would have gone out.

But there they were, all dressed in nautical attire, sun hats, slacks and deck
shoes, their faces smiling in anticipation—so I yielded, helped them aboard
and promised myself to keep a weather eye on that squally area. The Bay of St.
Louis is about five miles long and two miles wide at it narrowest, where the
train and car bridges cross. Outside of the bridges, the bay empties into the
Mississippi Sound, formed by the barrier islands, and then into the Gulf of
Mexico.

As we left the harbor, the sky above us was beautiful and disarming, and
once out on the bay, I was no longer apprehensive, though occasionally, I
would glance to the South where the dark clouds still persisted. The wind was a
little northerly and, while sailing East across the bay, the large mainsail hid the
southern sky, and the squall area. Squalls often skirted the bay, growling and
threatening, but many never actually struck. This optimism and lighthearted
conversation distracted me from caution.

We had sailed about two thirds of the way across the bay when the wind
began to increase and clock southerly, forcing me to tack, revealing a clear view
of the southern sky again. I was stunned. Those distant, dark clouds had raced
toward us without a sound. Now they were black, low-lying, ragged bottomed,
and moving rapidly to the North—and us. They appeared to be just South of
the bridge, less than a half mile away.

"Boy, I don't like the looks of that," I said, trying not to let my passengers
know just how concerned I really was. Aunt Alice and Nannette followed my
eyes, and at that same instant I saw what sailors fear most.

Just inside the bridge and less than two hundred yards from us, the surface
of the bay began to churn and swirl in a tight, frothy circle about fifteen feet in
diameter, and a misty column began to rise to the dark clouds above. I looked
up quickly and saw the silvery, dark funnel spiraling down.

Waterspout!

In seconds the tornado-like funnel descended to the surface of the water
joining the twisting, whipping spume and began sucking it into the sky, turning black and menacing as it filled with water. It grew rapidly to about thirty
feet in diameter and headed directly for us.

My thoughts raced inside my head bumping into each other while trying to
agree on what to do. We were closer to the eastern shore so I instinctively let
out the sail to a broad reach (my boat was strictly sail, no motor) and set a
course that would be at a right angle to the direction the waterspout was head-

ing in an attempt to avoid it. It was moving rapidly and I concentrated on trimming my sails to get the most speed I could out of the boat.

My mind seemed frozen, yet I managed to warn Aunt Alice and Nannette that should we capsize to hang onto the boat. My back was to the spout, but I could see by the girls' eyes as they grew wider and wider that it was getting closer.

I could hear it clearly now as it was about to pass off the stern of the boat, churning and whipping the air and water. It appeared for a moment as though I had avoided a direct collision, but the sound of wind and water increased and a sudden blast of wind struck the boat like a giant fist and flipped it over on its side—mast and sails in the water.

As the boat heeled over I automatically hiked out, which is instinctive to a sailor, but the girls simply tumbled out of the boat into the water.

In a brief second I saw Aunt Alice grab the base of the mast and wrap both arms around it. Good for her, I thought. What a gal. Poor Nannette, on the other hand, had nothing to hold on to and I saw her as she fell from the cockpit into the water and under the boat. I let go my grip on the rub-rail and went in after her, grabbed her around the waist and pulled her back into the cockpit, which was now beginning to fill with water.

I wasn't really concerned about the boat actually sinking. I felt sure I had installed ample Styrofoam floatation to keep it afloat but it had never really been tested, so I told the girls to put on life jackets.

Aunt Alice was ahead of me, already trying to put hers on, but she had picked up the child-sized jacket and, being a rather buxom woman, she was having a hard time "making ends meet."

The wind and rain were still with us, howling in our ears and pelting our faces. The girls appeared for the moment to be out of trouble, however, and my next thought was to attempt righting the boat. This was a particularly stupid thought as I look back now. Anyway, I swam around the stern of the boat to get to its bottom and the centerboard, pursuing the prescribed remedy for an overturned small sailboat. The centerboard was just the way I had hoped to find it, sticking straight out of the boat's bottom over the water. I hung all my weight on the centerboard with no effect and I guess I knew this wouldn't work, the boat was too full of water and the weight of two in the cockpit was too much but I had to try.

Giving that up, I began to swim back around the stern of the boat to check on the girls when two things happened that caused my mind to reel. First, I glanced to the north in the direction the waterspout had gone and through the driving rain I saw twin spouts in the center of the bay. My stomach felt funny and just at that moment, a terrified scream from the boat absolutely shattered whatever was left of my ability to think.

I tore at the water to get to the other side of the boat, not knowing what new calamity had occurred. To this day I don't know what happened to those other two spouts. My mind had switched to the more imminent problem.

As I thrashed around the stern I was greeted by another shriek and saw Nannette backed into the cockpit in water about chest high. She was screaming and beating the water directly before her and appeared to be trying to push something away from her. Her face was pure fright.

Then I saw it. My mind cracked. It was right in front of her less than a foot away. My God! The thing was roughly round and dark and about two feet across with long, undulating tentacles and was attacking her! I lunged toward Nannette with two or three swift strokes and was on top of the creature in seconds. I raised my right fist and punched with all my strength at the center of its body. There was no resistance as my fist and arm shot through its tentacles. I felt it clinging to my arm and jerked my arm out of the water. It was stuck to me, wrapped around my wrist and tangled in my watch. I shook my arm violently but unsuccessfully to rid myself of it. Then I heard Nanette shouting at me.

"Ray! Ray, it's my wig!"

"Wig?... *Wig*?!" I shouted. I looked at Nannette and then at the "creature" as it hung lifeless, its wet hairs still clinging to my arm. It was a time to laugh but the thought didn't even occur to me.

The boat was still sinking deeper into the water and I wondered if my do-it-yourself floatation would keep us afloat, or would it go to the bottom leaving us stranded in the middle of the bay with Aunt Alice still trying to put on that tiny life jacket and Nannette with the glazed stare of a soldier just back from the front lines.

As I recall, Aunt Alice and Nannette finally had their life jackets on and the boat had apparently sunk as far as it was going to. It lay on its side about two thirds submerged with the mast resting on the bottom of the bay about ten feet down.

Unknown to us, two young men in a motorboat, had witnessed our plight. They had sought refuge from the waterspout under the four-lane concrete bridge of highway 90, and as soon as the spout had gone they motored over and offered to help. I asked if they would take the girls to the yacht club and tell them I needed help and to please notify the Coast Guard Auxiliary.

After the motorboat left with the girls, I began trying to secure what equipment was still in the boat and gather what I could that was floating around in the water. I was pretty tired by now and decided it best to put on a life jacket myself.

It was at this time I noticed my plug rudder, tiller and all, was missing. When the boat had turned over on its side, the plug rudder and tiller had apparently slid out and gone to the bottom.

I would need to be towed. I felt that once the girls had gotten to the club, someone would probably come to help and of course I had asked for the Coast Guard also. Shortly, I saw a thirty-five to forty-foot motor launch coming out into the bay at the eastern shore near the mouth of Wolf River, one of several tributaries to the bay. As the yacht approached I saw two men in uniform; ties, caps—Coast Guard Auxiliary attire. One was coiling a line; the other had the helm in one hand and a pipe in the other. He was wearing sunglasses and his appearance was strongly reminiscent of a naval Admiral. He looked cool, composed and … dry.

He circled my drowning sailboat while giving commands to his companion, who had picked up a line with a float attached at one end and threw it to me. The "Admiral" then hailed me to grab the line and tie it to the top of the mast and he would right my "vessel."

Trying to maintain my dignity and act the part of the experienced sailor, I hailed back, "Yes, sir." Then it dawned on me that the top of the mast lay somewhere between eight and twelve feet down in the water and probably stuck in the mud. But I didn't hesitate. I meant to impress the Admiral and his crew.

I grabbed the line at the float end and placed it between my teeth in Tarzan fashion. I swam away from the boat until I judged I was approximately over the spot where the mast should be and then plunged under water.

I was doing a sort of breaststroke as I went beneath the water, using all the strength of my arms to reach the bottom as quickly as possible to conserve my breath. It was somewhat of a shock, therefore, to discover that I was going nowhere. Pull as I might with my arms and kicking as hard as I could with my legs and feet, I got no more than a couple of feet beneath the surface of the water. The damn life jacket. I forgot I was wearing the life jacket!

I bobbed back to the surface. I must have looked something like a fat duck feeding in a shallow pond, with its head beneath the water and its feet above. Embarrassed, and smiling weakly, I glanced at the Admiral. He had removed his pipe and was just standing there shaking his head from side to side. His partner, however, was much less considerate as he doubled over with laughter. Then I laughed also, at least I tried to.

I removed the jacket and tied it to the port shroud and forsaking any pretense of impressing the Admiral any longer, I swam back out over the water above the sunken mast and dove, this time successfully.

I dove just a few feet from the boat where I could see the mast as it entered the water, grabbed it and pulled myself hand over hand all the way down until I felt mud where the mast lay imbedded. I made a good, quick tie around the mast and swam again to the surface and popped a salute to the Admiral. He acknowledged, and mouthing a couple of commands to his assistant, began motoring upwind 180 degrees from the direction the mast was laying with the idea of pulling it vertical, thus righting the sailboat.

As the line tightened the boat began to slowly lift upright, the mast emerging from the water. It looked like it was going to be a successful maneuver. Yet, something from the dim past of experience warned me that this wasn't going to work. A vague recollection of attempting to right a water-filled sailboat before kept trying to tell me something. What had happened?

Then, as the mast lifted out of the water and rose to a vertical position, I remembered what had happened before. The mast simply continued past the vertical, fell into the water in the other direction, and back to the muddy bottom. The Admiral and I looked at each other—it was time for a conference.

I swam to the yacht and we decided it would be best to tow the boat to shore and bail it out before attempting to right it. I suggested that he pull the mast up again to the surface and let me tie a life jacket or two at the top to stop it from sinking. Then I would tie his towline to my bow eye and away we'd go to the shore.

The Admiral seemed quite surprised that I was able to contribute anything toward solving the problem. Having agreed on this procedure, the rest of the story is history and hard work. I was finally towed to shallow water where I returned the towline to the Admiral. And then, gesturing a farewell with his pipe, he smiled and motored away. A member of the yacht club eventually arrived and towed the boat and me back to the harbor

This was an experience no one in his right mind would ever intentionally undergo, yet, now that it is behind me, I relish it as one of my most adventurous sea stories.

Then It Happened

(Based on a True Story)

Mannheim, Germany 1958.

Something was ringing in the distance.

I reached out and smacked the alarm button. The ringing didn't stop. The telephone. I jumped out of bed glancing at the clock—two-thirty. What a hell of a time to call a practice alert.

Every month it was the same thing. You never knew what hour of the day or night it would come. Practice alerts were routine in the European Command and were designed to keep the troops on their toes in the event of war.

Trying not to disturb Peg and the children I made my way quickly through the darkness to the phone and picked up the receiver. "Lieutenant Allison speaking."

Almost before I had finished answering, an excited voice broke in, "This is the Battalion Duty NCO, sir. We've just received a USAREUR Alert—not a practice, the real thing,! All personnel are ordered to report immediately." My head spun and a sickening sensation rose from the pit of my stomach.

"Lieutenant Allison, sir, are you still there?"

"Yes … yes, sergeant, I'm here."

"Did you understand the message, sir?"

"Yes, I did, sergeant, I'll be right in."

My mind was suddenly jammed with questions. What had happened? Were we attacked? Would it mean all out war? Would Peg and the children be able to manage?

We had four beautiful children: Janie, age four, Mark, three, Cindy, two and Terry, nine months. I finally came to my senses and realized how much had to be done and how little time there was to do it.

I started back through the hallway and as I passed the children's rooms, tears came to my eyes. The apartment was still in darkness and quiet. All at once I felt small and incapable. Three thousand miles from home in a foreign country and war. The word seemed incongruous and unreal. Germany was a beautiful, picturesque country, especially here along the Rhine River. It had been a wonderful tour of duty and at times I had felt more like a civilian touring the world rather than a combat engineer. But now …

Gently, I nudged Peg. Her eyes opened slowly and I waited a few moments before speaking. Somehow after telling Peg I felt stronger and more competent. I was no longer cowered by the prospect of war but had assumed the role of protector.

Peg paled and her eyes moistened. "You'll have to leave right away, won't you?"

"As soon as I'm dressed," I answered.

"I had better get the children and myself dressed and ready," she said. There wouldn't really be that much packing for any of us. USAREUR (United States Army Europe) regulations required that the families of military personnel have a specified amount of food, clothing and other necessities packed at all times and the gas in the car was never allowed to be less than a half a tank. Routes of dependent withdrawal and a complete plan of evacuation had already been arranged, always with the hope that it would never be used.

We were both beginning feel the full impact now and our minds were too clouded with troubled thoughts of the future to make conversation.

My driver would be arriving shortly and I was trying to hurry. Yet I knew that each movement was taking me farther away from those I cherished. I wondered when I would see Peg and the children again. I finished dressing and was gathering the last of my equipment while Peg had gone into one of the children's rooms and turned on the light …

Then it happened!

The darkness outside suddenly turned to blinding, brilliant daylight. Peg screamed. Instinctively, I lunged down the hall toward Peg. The building lurched like a ship in a violent sea and the lights went out. I stumbled to the floor with large chunks of plaster falling about me. There was a shattering of glass mixed with the cries of Peg and the children. I thought of Terry and Cindy in the other bedroom.

The floor tilted about thirty degrees and the walls and ceiling of the apartment crumbled and fell to the street. Through the opening I could see the apartment across the street collapsing. The sky and everything beneath it was a weird shimmering cloud of thick red dust. The room heaved and twisted, walls tumbled, the floor split open and the four-story building fell with a thundering crash.

I could hear the screams of men, women and children mixed with the caving, crushing building. Terrible blows pounded and hammered at my body. Something crashed against my head ...

I could hear someone crying. Then there were others—screaming, wailing. God! They sounded like souls in hell. I was conscious but everything was dark and I couldn't move. I was buried. Something liquid and hot was running down my face. I could feel the same sensation on my chest, arms and right leg. I thought first it might be the broken hot water lines, but sharp thrusts of pain made me aware of the truth. I was bleeding.

Someone was calling my name. It was Peg and she was crying uncontrollably. Thank God. She was alive. Her cries were soon lost in the din of many others. For a moment, I thought I heard Janie's voice among them and as I thought of the children my heart almost burst.

I strained every muscle in my body to move and the pain increased. I managed to work my arms loose and was amazed to find them not broken. I began to claw at the bricks and rubble above me. My anxiety for Peg and the children drove me while the sharp edges of the broken bricks and concrete tore and split my fingers. The screams and cries mounted and joined until they became one horrible agonizing sound. As I dug, my hand suddenly grasped another. It was large and sticky and cold—it had no body. I was sick. Continuing to work my way upward I encountered other objects, some familiar, some not: rugs, lamps, chairs, books. At times I felt faint and had to stop. Finally, one hand broke free into the cool night air and then the other. I removed the last remaining obstacles, pulled my body clear and breathed deeply.

For a moment I sat there stunned. I stared about me. It was like one huge rock pile. What had once been an American housing area for several thousand servicemen and their dependents was now a graveyard of crushed concrete, broken brick and splintered furniture for the dead, dying and mourning. Then, I saw Peg, less than thirty feet from me. She was half buried and holding Mark in her arms. Both were crying and covered with blood.

I rose shakily to my feet. My right leg hurt intensely and would hardly support me. I staggered and fell several times before reaching them.

As I drew close to Peg our eyes met. I shall never forget her expression. Her lips parted to say something, then tightened. My eyes followed hers as she looked down at Mark and a cold chill swept over me as my gaze fell on his legs.

They were twisted grotesquely as though made of clay. He was sobbing pitifully. Peg broke down completely. It seemed something was about to snap inside me, like a watch wound too tight.

Then, Peg abruptly stopped crying and stared at me. "The children!" she screamed. "The other children!" I turned quickly and began staggering about blindly. My mind was numb and it was all I could do to think coherently. Where? For God's sake, where do I look? In addition to the confusion of destruction, most of the furniture in the apartments was the same.

Army vehicles were beginning to arrive at the edge of the area, casting their headlights across the writhing mountain of humanity and destruction. All about me people were stumbling around screaming and crying for loved ones and occasionally, there were the wails of those who had found them. It was a hideous nightmare.

As the lights began to pierce the chaos and dust, I saw more and more lifeless bodies. I retraced my steps to the place I had been buried. Moving across the debris to where the children's room might have fallen, I began removing pieces of brick and concrete. As I bent over, my eyes froze on an object a short distance from me. It was the hand of a child. It looked out of place and unreal amid the destruction. Nothing seemed real anymore. Then the little hand moved. I fell to my knees and began removing the broken brick. The pajamas. They were Janie's pajamas! I dug frantically and from below I heard a soft sobbing.

In a few minutes, with both my hands bleeding, I stumbled toward Peg with a limp, but breathing, crying child in my arms. If I hadn't been Janie's father, I never would have recognized her. "Oh merciful God!" cried Peg, as she saw Janie. I laid her on Peg's lap. She was caked with blood and plaster dust. Peg noticed a partly buried sheet and asked for it.

I knelt by Peg and held her hand. Tears were streaming from her eyes as she began to clean and bandage the children. I rose to my feet again and began looking for Cindy and Terry. There was more light now. Generators had arrived and bright searchlights aided in the rescue and evacuation. Medics with stretchers and Geiger counters were moving about the area, checking radiation levels and carrying their pitiful cargo. On a clear section of the street, a long still line of humanity was being laid out and covered with blankets and sheets.

I continued searching, estimating as best I could where the other bedroom might have fallen and began digging. I found a couple and their child who lived above us on the fourth floor—they were dead. I helped another officer remove his wife from beneath a refrigerator. Both her legs were smashed but she was alive. I was sick to my stomach frequently and my throat was raw.

It was hopeless, I told myself. It had been blind fortune to find Janie and a miracle to find her alive. I was so weak now I could barely lift one foot in front of the other and my arms were limp. I had stopped bleeding, however, and the pain in my right leg had settled into numbness. I wandered about in a daze, too tired to really concentrate on my search but too heartbroken to give up.

Then I saw it—a little red slipper. I stumbled quickly toward it and picked it up. I recognized the mending on the toe that little Terry had worn through. My hands began to claw and tear at the debris. In order to lift some of the larger pieces of concrete I had to use the leg of a table as a lever.

A few minutes later I had uncovered a blood-stained bed and a small, life-less body, I bit my lips until they bled. It was Terry. Her little face had somehow not been marred but was covered with dirt. Kneeling, I gently cleaned it with my hand. I didn't bring Terry to her mother. Just a few feet away I saw the splintered frame of a baby bed. I was crying now and made no effort to stop. In another few minutes there were two small bodies before me. My eyes began to burn as I said a prayer.

Someone had walked up and stood beside me. It was my driver and platoon sergeant. I rose slowly to my feet and looked back toward Peg and the children. A medic had arrived and was attending them. I turned to my sergeant and asked if the battalion had moved out yet.

"No, sir," he replied. "We're not going to move out."

I looked at him questioningly.

"The war is over, sir. We won."

I looked at the destruction about me, then back at the sergeant.

"Won what, sergeant?"

He didn't answer. I glanced at my watch. It was four-thirty.

"In the Beginning ..."

It was noon on a hot August day as I drove beneath the archway. The white letters, following the curve of the black wrought iron, lay accented against the dark green and gray of the moss-covered oaks beyond ... "Oaklawn Cemetery."

It appeared to be a cool shady place to eat the lunch my wife had prepared for me. I always tried to find a place that would offer some refuge from the heat of the day as well as the turbulence of city traffic; a place to reflect, to seek answers, to take stock of one's life. A place to take the time to think about things that life's busy routine seldom allowed, a pause in our rush to the grave. I don't mean to sound morbid, but I do feel that in the final analysis, it is death that holds the real answers to our questions about life.

There was a subtle magnetism here. The shade of the large trees was inviting and provided a feeling of relief as I drove in and parked under a huge old oak that spread its moss-covered limbs over me like the wings of an old mother hen.

I turned off the motor and rolled down the windows. A quiet, pervading calm surrounded me. The sounds of the busy world had retreated into the muffled distance.

My eyes began to randomly scan the graves, the tombstones and vaults, and the names inscribed on them. I wondered what their lives had been like, what had they learned through death, what they could tell us now, were they able.

It was a different world here and for some reason, I sensed I was somehow intruding ... a peculiar thought. There was no apparent reason for this other than the contrast to the hustle and bustle of the noisy city from which I had managed to escape briefly. I dismissed the feeling and began to eat my lunch.

A slight breeze gently disturbed the gray moss that hung like ragged shrouds from the heavy-boned limbs of the massive oak ... that wasn't exactly a pleasant imagery, I thought to myself.

I finished my lunch and relaxed, soaking up the solitude. The feeling of intruding persisted, however. I felt like someone was watching me. I actually twisted around in my seat, and looked, really expecting to see someone. Nothing. I felt a little stupid and lay back against the headrest and closed my eyes.

What was that? I opened my eyes, sat up and looked around again. I was sure I had heard someone. Then something startling occurred. Nothing had outwardly changed, yet I was suddenly dumbfounded by thoughts forming in my mind—but they were not my thoughts! I sat as in a trance, mesmerized by what was happening.

"What do you want of us?"

My mind froze. I had not thought that. That wasn't me!

It was like hearing a strange voice in a dark room. My lips attempted to form an exclamation but I could not utter a word. My physical self seemed paralyzed by an alien invasion of my mind. My thoughts stammered several unspoken questions.

"What? Who are you? Where are you?" I heard my questions but I had not spoken them.

"That's so typical of you people, always distracted and scatterbrained. Which question do you wish me to answer first? You must learn to concentrate and control your thoughts. One question at a time."

I sat stunned. Whatever doubt I had about what was happening fled before the stark reality of the voice inside my head. "I don't believe this." I thought. "Who are you?"

"There you go again. Who I am is really of little consequence. *That* I am, however, should be worthy of your consideration. I do, nevertheless, appreciate your incredulity. Most of you who have managed to crossover react pretty much the same."

I tried to get a grip on my thoughts, to calm the explosion in my mind that seemed to have blown away my reasoning. I tried to comprehend what was occurring.

"Now, that's better. You are adapting very well, all things considered. You have a fine mind. Too bad you don't put it to better use more often. You are very capable of thought conversation once you accept that we are real."

"We?" Part of my mind seemed to have grasped something that began to calm the storm of disbelief clouding my thoughts.

"Of course 'we'—all of us here."

"You mean you're one of the ... of the ..." as I thought of all the graves about me.

"Certainly, who did you think I was?"

"I don't know. I'm not really sure what I think about all this."

The more accustomed I became to his thoughts, the less strange they sounded. They were becoming familiar, almost friendly. Now, only a small part of my mind still scampered about looking for a place to hide, refusing to accept what was happening.

"What are you doing here?"

"Come now, you have known the answer to that since Sunday school, or Catechism, whichever has been your preference. We are waiting, of course."

"Waiting? For what?"

"For the same thing you are, only in our state we think of little else. In your world, with all its distractions, it is much more difficult for you to think about, shall I say, 'the bottom line,' such as 'where did I come from and where am I going?"

"Why haven't I heard of anything like this happening before?"

"You haven't heard of this before because the others, like you, who have thought with us, have been reluctant to tell anyone else, just as you will be. I'm afraid you would be considered ... you know, not right in the head. Am I correct?"

"Yes, I suppose you're right, but how does this happen?" I seemed to have much more control of my thoughts now and found it easier to converse and to analyze objectively.

"You learn fast. Your thought control is unusual for someone with so little experience in thought conversation, but don't be too prideful. It has more to do with an accident of your 'schematics' rather than any super intelligence or effort on your part. People are different, you know."

"You mentioned 'we.' If there are others, why do I hear only you?"

"Because, if you could hear all of us, it would sound something like this ..."

Suddenly, into my mind burst the sounds of voices: gentle murmuring, laughter, hideous angry cries, anguished wailing, pitifully sad moaning and whimpering. I thought my head was going to explode.

"Stop!" I screamed in thought. And it stopped.

"You can understand now, why it is better to limit the conversation to just the two of us."

"How did you do that? Why do I hear only you now?"

"That will be a little more difficult to explain, since I am not quite sure myself except that you 'touched' me with your thoughts and I locked in' on your mind. It's a chance occurrence, but that is why right now you cannot move a muscle. I have 'frozen' you to my mind only, and once I release you, the likelihood of your ever re-establishing contact with me or our world again will be very remote.

"Our minds are very similar," he went on, "sort of like being on the same wavelength, but if I allow a slight variance, left or right, you can hear the rest of my world. It's like tuning a radio. If not set correctly, you receive more than one station. In most cases, a crossover is an accident, though there have been exceptions. There have been some from your world, who have possessed the mental power to enter our world with no help from us."

I thought about this, and the mystics and clairvoyants I had heard about from time to time, and wondered.

"The voices I heard, some sounded in pain and others were laughing and crying … some were horrible …?"

"They're people, individuals, with their own ideas about where they are and where they are going. Many are happy, some are terrified of what they expect to happen."

"And what is going to happen?" I was increasingly calmer and now fascinated by the opportunity to learn all that I could from this unique experience.

"I told you we were alike, you and I. You are not one to panic and I'd like to think the same of myself. But, as much as I would like to answer that question, I can't. You see, I, or we, I should say, know little more than you do about what the future holds. But there is a difference. While on your side, in your world, we doubted, just like you, if there was anything after death. Well, we know now there is, because here we are, on the other side. We are aware of the transition.

"The non-material 'life' we live is in itself proof that 'the grave is not our goal.' We are convinced now that more is to follow in the Designer's good time."

"Designer?"

"Whatever you want to call it. Certainly you don't think, like some, that all this is a chance happening, do you?"

"No, but I can't say that I have really been able to grasp the significance of it all either. I have tried but there are too many conflicting beliefs."

"What do you believe, *now?*"

I hesitated. "Well, *until now,* I had reasoned that perhaps I was just a part of the infinity of space, part of something that had no beginning or ending. In this there was, at least to some extent, a sense of perpetuation and a resignation to whatever form I might be relegated in the process of dying. I thought that though I might not continue after death as an independent, thinking being, neither would I cease entirely to exist.

"I might become part of a flower, a cloud or a mountain stream, or what-ever, but I would continue as part of the universe. This has been my minimal expectancy. To what extent my sense of self would survive death, however, I could not predict. It was with acquiescence, therefore, with concession and a sense relief, without fear, that I felt I would like to accept death, to know that I would always be a part of the future. This was only my conjecture, of course, a substitute for the truth for which I have been searching. This experience with you has, of course, changed things considerably and I am still trying to com-prehend its significance."

For the first time, he was silent, as though considering something. I waited.

Finally, he began again, slowly choosing his words.

"I should tell you that there is more, exceedingly more, for you to experi-ence while this opportunity exists, but I must also caution you there is a risk involved.

"There are greater thought perceptions of which we are capable that you are not, at least not without our help. Our ability to experience these strange insights appears to be a way of preparing us for the ultimate purpose of our existence—a never ending world of perfect thought with 'the Designer'—per-fect thought and therefore, perfect comprehension and contentment.

'The reason I say that this is done at some risk is because some from your side have not been able to withstand such thoughts or revelations and their minds have been irrevocably damaged by the experience, or, let's say, their 'schematics' were short-circuited by the overload.

"And, though I warn you of the danger, I must also emphasize that the opportunity you have is a rare one. Few people from your side will ever have the chance to perceive the world in such depth and truth. It's really up to you, however, and should you elect to experience this, it will necessarily end our contact with each other."

A chance to perceive the truth. Without hesitation, without a sound, my mind consented.

"Then I will say good-bye to you now. If you endure, profit by what you experience. And, you must also realize, that should you survive, more will be expected of you as a consequence of this knowledge."

At the last moment I questioned my decision, but the thought had not formed clearly enough to stop what occurred ...

Total darkness. Complete silence. Limitless dimension and a feeling of movement—of extreme acceleration through space, in all directions at once, never ending. An infinite exploration—infinity and eternity the same. No beginning, no ending. I was in a huge void, yet, its singularity constituted a "presence" in itself. I could feel it—feel the hidden power in its vastness, a power that dwarfed the infinity that it permeated and in which I existed. It was as if I also existed through all of space, that I extended forever, that I was a part of this power and it a part of me.

And yet, I was apart, detached, as though I was an observer, discovering, being led to discover. Being led? Yes, that was the feeling. I was being led, shown.

This was what existed before anything was. And yet, something was there ... I sensed it. I felt dwarfed, minute. There was a purpose, a meaning—an intelligence. It was aware of me, and I felt a warmth, a caring. I felt *love*. I did not want it to end. I wanted to go on forever, just like this.

Then suddenly, a gigantic, cosmic explosion of blinding, white-hot light shattered into trillions of parts, and raced through the "presence" and the feeling of a "power" was overwhelming.

I seemed to be all places at once within the light, its center and its extremities, as it penetrated the infinite darkness, darkness so unending that it would never be totally aware of the light ... an impossible thought?

I perceived the tangible and the intangible. I saw the macro and the micro ... the dividing and subdividing into myriad parts, growing smaller and smaller, then combining, forming, growing larger and larger, all with design and purpose.

It was a wonderful sensation, a beautiful spectacle. I was completely overcome by euphoria. I began within infinity, a tangible within the intangible. The tangible was enormous, and yet, minuscule compared to the intangible that had preceded it.

Everything gave bold, irrefutable testimony to the essence of that intangibility ... of the "Presence." My being seemed to burst with understanding. I knew.

And then, I heard a voice from deep in the darkness, insistent, and I was racing through space, contracting, returning. The voice persisted, and the blackness and the vastness and exploding light disappeared as I opened my eyes.

"I'm really sorry to bother you, but they're due here any minute. I have to ask you to move. You're blocking the drive. They're going to need room to park, you know, the funeral"

"Oh, sure," I said, "must've dozed off." My shirt was soaked with sweat. The sun had changed. The shade was gone. "I need to go anyway," I said, trying to adjust to the sudden reality of where I was and where I had been.

I started the car, rolled up the windows, turned on the air conditioning and drove out through the archway, just as a long line of cars was about to turn in. I watched in my rearview mirror as they drove onto the shell drive and into the cemetery.

I turned my eyes back to the road before me, back to my world, my magnificent, beautiful world, I marveled at its existence—and my own.

The Gate

Hurriedly, I laced my sneakers, skipping every other hole. It was a perfect day. The sky was a brilliant clear blue. A brisk autumn wind frolicked among the branches of the tall pines and seemed to beckon for a playmate. I could hear its excited whispers squeezing through the ill-fitted window frames with eager impatience, "Hurry, Jimmy, hurry!" I picked up the kite and admired it.

It was the finest I had ever made, a five sticker, including a fighter lance and hummer. A red starburst stood out boldly on a background of white tissue, drawn tight by sprinkling with water and holding it over the floor furnace to dry. Red and white streamers fell gracefully from both ends of the belly stick and the slender tip of the lance.

It had a twenty-foot tail, made from an old red tablecloth that Mrs. Raum had given me, and matched the color of the starburst perfectly. I rolled it into a tight, neat ball, picked up my kite string and raced down the steps two at a time.

Mrs. Raum and the other grownups were in the large dining room. The kitchen ladies in their blue uniforms were serving breakfast and the two nurses dressed in white were sitting at a table by themselves.

They were all looking at me with those stupid, grown-up looks, all except Mrs. Raum. Somehow, she was different. There was a tender warmth about her even when she chided me.

"Jimmy, you know you're not supposed to run down the stairs like that, I'm so afraid you're going to fall and hurt yourself."

"I'm sorry, Mrs. Raum, I'll try to remember," I said, moving toward the door.

"And just where do you think you're going with that kite?"

"The wind is perfect, Mrs. Raum, and I …"

"Jimmy, you haven't even had your breakfast yet, and have you forgotten that the doctor and your mother are coming to see you this morning?"

"I don't want to see him." I said quickly, knowing that I would have to. "Why does he have to come with my mother?"

Two of the old ladies looked up and clacked their tongues in admonition. I loved my mother but there was something about the doctor that scared me, that made me think of things I didn't like to think about.

Mr. Raum walked in from the kitchen wearing a soiled white apron. He glanced quickly at his wife and then at me. "Well, Jimmy, how about some hot cakes and sausage and a big glass of milk?" He turned to his wife and gave her that look he always did when I was around. "If you hurry, you'll be finished before your mom gets here." He acted funny and looked at Mrs. Raum again.

Mr. Raum was always acting, he never said what he meant; always hiding something. I never knew what and it made me angry. He thinks he fools me and that makes me even angrier.

"I don't want to eat. I don't want to see him!" I shouted, and bolted for the door. I saw Mr. Raum start for me but Mrs. Raum reached out and held his arm and as she looked at him, I thought for a moment she too was hiding something.

Several of the old men were on the porch and I almost collided with one in a wheelchair as I lunged down the steps and across the expanse of lawn that stretched nearly a quarter mile to the gate.

As I looked at the gate I stopped running. She would come, all right. Every Wednesday she came, and she would bring the doctor with her. The doctor always came with her. During the week he comes alone and talks to me. He talks like Mr. Raum and he thinks he is fooling me too. He also has a secret and I can tell that he has told my mother, but I don't care. They can keep their old secrets.

The men in uniform were at the gate. They were always at the gate. They look like policemen but they aren't. They have secrets too. Who cares about their old secrets?

I looked at the gate and the tall long fence that grew out of both sides. I wondered about it and tried to remember when I had come through it. I couldn't. Maybe I had always been here. Somehow that wasn't right but I could not recall ever having been anyplace else. There was something wrong about that and I tried to think about it.

I felt the chill wind stiffen and nudge me, like the nose of a playful horse. I forgot the gate and watched the wind as it skimmed across the great lawn.

Myriad blades of grass bowed in impulsive tribute as the Prince of Nature swept by. I wish that I were the wind, free to race over the earth or zoom into the sky, to push the clouds and play with the birds.

I looked at the fence and the thick, green hedges that grew against it and wondered if he would be there today. It was a world of secrets and I felt smug that I had so cleverly guarded mine. I strained to see into the dark shadows that fell from the hedges.

I looked around. There was no one, only the men at the gate and they never paid any attention to me unless I got too close to the gate.

I tied my string to the kite's bridle and loosened its long flame of red tail. It tugged anxiously at my hand, the hummer already beginning its staccato bumblebee sound. I began to run toward the fence and slacken out string. The kite climbed proudly into the sky, its fighter stick, menacing and sharp, pierced the bright blue; its long red tail falling like a stream of crimson blood across the sky.

When I reached the bushes I sat down with my back close against them and began to let out more string. I had rolled two spools of 100 yard No. 8 white thread onto a piece of sturdy, smooth oak branch, and holding each end loosely cupped between the thumb and index finger of my hands, the string whirred off I stopped it periodically, letting the string tighten, causing the kite to climb higher and higher and farther and farther away until the red starburst on its breast was only a blur.

I looked about again. Satisfied no one was watching, I spoke over my shoulder.

"Are you there, Mickey?"

"Yeah, man. Boy, that's a real beaut' you got up there today, Jimmy. I can't wait to get the feel of that baby." A small lump of shadow all at once came to life inside the bushes and moved close to me, carefully avoiding the searching eye of the sun.

"Are you ready?" I asked

"You bet." A young hand reached out anxiously.

"Be careful now and hold 'er tight. Lot of wind up there today. And watch those trees over there if she dives."

"O.K., right."

Mickey chattered for a while and then grew silent, mesmerized by the kite's lofty antics.

I lay on my back staring at the sky, watching the clouds twist and float past, which made the kite appear to soar across the sky like a comet. The impression was so real that I looked and checked the string, only to find it still and unaffected by the kite's imaginary flight across the heavens.

All at once, Mickey's urgent whisper interrupted.

"Jimmy. Jimmy, look!"

From the corner of my eye I saw what appeared to be two giants, their heads high against the sky, smiling down at me. I quickly sat up, grabbing the kite string from Mickey who immediately disappeared with a rustle into the bushes and through our secret hole in the fence.

"Hello, Jimmy. That's a mighty fine kite you have there."

She was beautiful, I thought. Her hair was soft and bright as gold, like a piece of the sun fallen to earth. Her eyes were like the blue of the sky I had been watching only a moment before. They seemed to search, to seek out a part of me that only she knew was there, and something stirred inside me, a feeling, remote—of something I had known long ago ... before the gate.

The doctor stood behind her watching me. Soon he would start asking those questions again. Finally, he spoke. "Do you mind if we sit down with you for awhile, Jimmy?" Not waiting for an answer, they both stretched out on the grass beside me. "How old are you now, Jimmy?" he asked looking up at the kite.

"Eleven," I said reluctantly, and watched them look at each other like they always did when I answered their questions.

"My but you're a big boy for eleven, aren't you?" He looked at me.

I was big and there seemed to be something wrong about that. It made me feel ashamed somehow, even with Mickey. I tried to think about it.

"Do you like flying kites, Jimmy?" he asked, looking at the kite again.

"Yes," I said, giving the string a couple of angry jerks that sent the kite into a shallow dive. His questions always annoyed me, always made me think things I didn't want to think.

"What would you like to be when you grow up, Jimmy?"

"I want to build airplanes," I said quickly, surprising myself, and felt strange because I could not remember thinking of that before—yet there seemed to be something familiar about it.

They looked at each other briefly and I could tell by their faces that what I had said had touched close to their secret. They smiled at each other.

"Like that one up there?" he asked, pointing to the sky behind us.

It was as if he had planned it. I looked behind me and as my eyes found the huge airliner, something grabbed at my mind and caught hold, and forced me to think. The sight of the large aircraft seemed all at once to dwarf the world around me, to diminish the reality of everything else. It was like a giant fixation point.

I studied the plane, the sweep of its wings, the sleek length of its body, the power of its two vapor spewing jet engines. I felt suddenly drawn into a part of my mind that had been closed to me.

Sudden flashes of images that were at the same time strange and familiar superimposed themselves across the plane in the sky—a drawing board, T-square, protractors, fuel consumption calculators, logarithmic tables, wind velocity, lift computations …

And then there was another plane in the sky. It was falling, out of control, plummeting to earth in a crazy, wobbling dive.

"My God! It's going to crash!" I heard myself scream, but it wasn't my voice. I saw the black billowing smoke push suddenly from the earth to the sky, pursued by monstrous tongues of flame. For an instant there was an unreal silence, then came the deafening explosion—and then it was gone.

I jumped to my feet. The kite string dropped to the ground, the oak branch skittering and tumbling wildly across the grass until the kite sank into the distant trees and was gone. "Kate! Kate, I killed them!" I cried. My chest heaved and I felt tears streaming down my face, mixing with the cold sweat of horror.

"No, Jim, no. It wasn't your fault, honey. The investigation proved that. Jim, you must believe it. It wasn't your fault." I felt her arms holding me tight, her small head against my chest.

She was crying. And then with a rush it came, with all the pain and agony, and there were no longer any secrets.

"It's all right, Kate, it's all right," I said, gently stroking her soft golden hair and holding her close to me. I looked at the doctor.

"Welcome back, Jim", he said smiling, "Welcome back."

The guard swung the gate open and the car passed.

"Say, wasn't that the crackpot that's been flying those kites in here for the last few weeks?"

"That's the guy who's been flying kites, all right, but he's no crackpot. That's Jim Reichert, the nation's top jet designer. Cracked up after one of his newest planes crashed on its maiden flight last month. Thought it was his fault. Turned out to be pilot error."

"Who was the blonde with him?"

"His wife."

A Final Resolution

I sat up on the edge of my bed, still groggy from a restless night. Automatically, I reached for the cigarettes and lighter on the night table. As I picked up the open pack, the aroma of tobacco teased my nostrils and intensified the craving in the pit of my stomach. The thumb of my right hand began feverishly spinning the little wheel across the worn flint of my old Zippo lighter in a vain effort to produce a flame. Suddenly, the wheel spun free as the last remnant of flint disappeared.

Growing irritated by the futility of my efforts and the failure to abate the surging desire for a smoke, I tried to recall where I had placed my extra flints. Try as I did to concentrate, however, my thoughts were persistently interrupted by an unreasonable impatience for "relief from the leaf." Matches. There must be matches here somewhere. I checked the chest of drawers, coat pockets, pants pockets, desk drawers, medicine cabinet and pantry—all refused to reveal the whereabouts of flint or sulfur. My irritation progressed rapidly to loss of temper and became manifest as I began slamming drawers shut and flinging the useless garments about the room, while the cigarette, growing soggy between my lips, dangled ineffectually.

A fierce anger grew within me and giving vent to its frustrated rage I kicked the closet door shut with a mighty boot from my shoeless right foot. The impact reverberated loudly through the apartment, accented by a sudden howl that did justice to the excruciating pain of smashed toes.

The noisy, drawer-slamming search continued (minus kicking) punctuated by brief, vile testimonials to the lousy, rotten, inefficient world I lived in. All this conjuring, however, produced not a single flame. The thought of procuring a light from my neighbor across the hall occurred to me but I couldn't bring myself to admit publicly that I couldn't "take 'em or leave 'em."

Yanking the cigarette from my mouth, I winced and cursed again as a sharp pain stabbed at both lips where dried saliva had cemented the paper to the delicate membranes. This incident provided the spark that ignited an explosive mixture of frustration, guilt, desire and physical deterioration that had been brewing for the past twenty years at a rate of three packs a day.

With a howl of denunciation that sounded with the finality of Gabriel's horn, I screamed aloud a final resolution never to touch another damned cigarette as long as I lived—a resolution that I was destined to keep in spite of the past's shameful record of broken promises.

This time I was really ashamed of myself and realized the loss of self-respect that had accompanied these humiliating failures. I had debased my intellect through self-deceit, for I had long since reasoned the foolhardiness of smoking. I had always taken pride in myself as being a self-determined man but, when "the need for a weed" arose, or I was in "lack of a pack," it inevitably meant capitulation. I was the slave and tobacco the master. This fact gnawed at my manhood and rationalization had been my sole refuge. I had always been intelligent enough, however, to convince myself that I could "kick the habit" whenever I wanted to and somehow this conveniently justified my continued addiction.

My mind dwelled on the false pretenses under which I had smoked all these years, on the damage I had done to my character, to self-discipline, the dissipation of my body, the loss of taste and smell, the shortness of breath (and temper), sleepless nights and muddled thinking, and burnt holes in my new suits. As I realized these things my thoughts formed as an invincible army and delivered a deathblow to smoking with the most effective weapon known against a "nag for a fag"—will power.

This time I knew it was the real thing. This time I knew I would win. A feeling of overwhelming joy rose from my heart and I felt giddy at the prospect of winning this twenty-year war with nicotine.

In a burst of enthusiasm I felt the blood race through my veins and my heart pounded with elation. I experienced difficulty in breathing, my vision blurred—I couldn't swallow and something struck repeatedly at my chest. The floor spun and my head burst.

The death certificate indicated impassively, "Coronary Thrombosis" as the cause of death. What caused the coronary? The attending physician preferred not to think about that right now as he pressed the cigarette tightly between his lips and sucked deeply, allowing the smoke to mushroom into his lungs where, permeating tissue already blackened by its frequent passage, it continued into the blood stream, eventually to reach the heart.

The Race

(Based on a True Story)

The slate-gray squall was bearing down on us out of the North. I recognized all the danger signs, but my one-track sailor's mind filtered out all but the fact that we would get the wind first and still might catch the fleet. We were racing Flying Scots and were in last place.

Wally Brown was on the main and Phil Williams on the jib and spinnaker. The chances of catching the fleet were really remote but until the final gun is fired, you feel that anything can happen. Well, it did, but not at all what we expected.

As I said, we were in last place with all sails up and full, including the spinnaker. We were heading from the North mark to the South mark with the wind dead astern, when the first head winds of the squall rolled out across the bay and reached our boat. The Scot leaped forward and the water began to churn beneath her bow.

As the main body of the squall struck, the wind grew much stronger and I became concerned about capsizing. I wasn't worried about the physical danger to my crew or myself, only that if we turned over we would surely be out of the race. The race was everything. Neither my crew nor I gave even a cursory thought about the life jackets that lay forward in the bow of the boat; our attention was focused solely on how to make the boat go faster.

As the wind gusted the boat rocked and threatened to broach. Finally, my mind accepted the warning. I told Phil to take down the spinnaker. Just as he stood up, however, and reached for the spinnaker pole, an intense gust of wind punched at the sails. The boat abruptly heeled and kept right on heeling until it turned over on its side with mast and sails, and us, in the water.

We immediately executed the prescribed remedy for an overturned yacht. We swam around to the bottom of the boat, which was now floating on its side, grabbed the extending centerboard and pulled down with all our weight.

Wally and Phil actually climbed up on the board to bring their full weight to bear. Our efforts were timely and successful, the boat began to right, and the mast lifted from the water and rose to the upright position. It looked as though we might still catch the fleet.

As the boat righted, however, Wally and Phil fell from the centerboard back into the water several feet from the boat, and at about the same time, even stronger winds arrived. There was a sudden explosion of sails filling with wind and the boat bolted away like a frightened stallion. At the last second, I instinctively reached up and grabbed the port stay with both hands and suddenly found myself being dragged through the water and across the bay, leaving my crew behind.

It all happened so fast I didn't really have time to consider the consequences of what was occurring. The alternate billowing and collapsing of sails caused the boat to roll and heel erratically and the spinnaker, hooked over the top of the mast, kept filling and spewing air.

The racket of flapping, popping sails and banging sheets and blocks were accompanied by the howling wind, thunder and lightning, and a driving, blinding rain. It made it difficult to think. My mind seemed numbed by the trauma of the moment.

As the boat rocked back and forth from starboard to port in the wind and waves, I was plunged in and out of the water while still holding tightly to the stainless steel port shroud. The wire cable had begun to cut into my hands and wrist and I wondered just how long I could continue to hang on. I knew I had to do something. I had left my crew without life jackets stranded in the middle of the bay over a mile from shore. I had to get into the boat.

I made several attempts to pull myself out of the water and onto the slippery, fiberglass deck but was unable to get a firm grip anywhere. It was all I could do just to hold on, much less muster the energy to pull myself up that wet shroud and into the boat.

I thought of the safety line on the stern, slung between two stainless steel rings … but some of the boats had them and some didn't … If I let go and moved to the stern and it wasn't there—or if I missed it and lost the boat completely …? For a brief moment I wanted to yield to the temptation to just let go. I was hurting and I was tired, but kept reminding myself of my crew.

It had finally gotten to the point, however; where I was afraid I simply did not have the strength to hold on any longer. It was a scary time and on at least two occasions, when the boat rolled over, I almost lost my grip on the shroud. At one point, however, in an attempt to pull myself into the boat, one of my hands touched the spinnaker trim which lay along the surface of the deck … It might work, I thought, it just might work.

I let go with one hand and found the trim, pulled it down into the water and fashioned a large, stirrup-like loop and tied it in a good tight granny knot to the base of the shroud where it attached to the deck. Putting my left foot into the loop, I was able to haul myself up onto the boat.

I slipped on the wet deck and went sprawling into the cockpit slamming my leg against the centerboard casing. My leg went numb, then hurt like hell as the muscle knotted. The boat was still rocking and yawing and seemed even more determined to turn over again, now that my weight was no longer hanging over the high side to hold her down. Fear dug at my insides. If the boat should turn over again it would be the end of any chance I had of getting back to my crew.

I stumbled aft to the tiller and struggled to bring the boat about, which was made difficult because of the twisted entanglement of sheets and trims. The wind and angrily flapping sails had twisted them together in an impossible mess. It was all I could do to manhandle the stubborn tiller and bring the boat across the wind without turning over. With the boat finally about, I tried as best I could to sail back in the direction from which I had come.

The rain was so heavy I couldn't see more than twenty to thirty yards, but judging by the wind, I felt that I was returning pretty much in the direction from which I had come and where I had left my crew.

I kept trying to untangle the mainsheet in order to gain some control over the wind on the sail. The jib trims were hopelessly snarled and there was nothing I could do about the spinnaker since it was irretrievably hooked over the top of the mast. This posed the greatest threat to my remaining upright. Periodically, the huge sail would fill and balloon with air, tugging at the top of the mast and pulling it down toward the water, threatening to turn the boat over again.

It was really touch and go to remain afloat and at the same time to retrace my way back to my crew. Our guardian angels must have been working overtime, nevertheless, because shortly, I looked through the rain off the port bow and I saw a head bobbing in the water about thirty feet away. It was Wally Brown.

"How're you doing Wally?" I called out.

"Great. Absolutely great," was his reply. There was a touch of sarcasm, humor, relief … and unquestionable fatigue in his words.

I eased the boat near him and shouted, "Catch!" and threw him one of the life jackets that were now floating in the bilge of the boat. This had added to the problem of steering, for there were now a good six to eight inches of water sloshing from side to side and forward and aft.

"Have you seen Phil?" I yelled again.

"I saw him a little while ago but I don't see him now." Something tightened in my stomach. Had I lost him? "Hang on to that jacket. I'm going after him," I hollered. I had thought briefly about trying to haul Wally aboard, but to attempt that and still keep the boat upright would have been dangerous. It could have resulted in capsizing again which would have left Phil with no one to help him. I knew Wally was safe with the life jacket so I continued looking for Phil.

The rain had finally begun to abate somewhat, and visibility had increased. I held the same course and in less than a hundred feet, off the starboard side of the boat, I spotted Phil. He was on his back, his head just above the water, and he was periodically crying out for help. I don't recall now whether I saw him first or heard him first, but it was a smart thing for him to do for I could have missed him.

I yelled at Phil but since his head was mostly under water he couldn't hear me. The wind was still blowing hard as I guided the rocking, heeling boat as close to him as possible and then reached out and slammed a life jacket in his face to be sure it got his attention. Phil grabbed the jacket and his head popped out of the water.

"How you doing, buddy?"

"Fine" he said, "Just fine." and managed a smile.

"Put on that jacket. I'll get help".

The thought occurred to me again to try to pull him into the boat but I was afraid to leave the tiller for a second for fear the boat would turn over again, and frankly, I don't believe either of us would have had the strength to get him into the boat.

I hadn't realized I was in such poor shape. Every movement was a real physical effort. I had a hard time catching my breath and my mind seemed to have bogged down to simple moment-to-moment thoughts, without being quite sure what I was going to do next. I managed to jibe and started looking for one of the other sailboats, and help. The boat was yawing from side to side in considerable seas and heeling dangerously as the bilge water shifted from one side then to the other.

It was about this time I saw John Christensen and his crew come looming out of the rain. They had also turned over in the squall but had managed to successfully right their boat. I hailed John and told him what had happened, indicating where my crew was, and asked if he could take them aboard while I tried to limp our boat back to the club. It was with great relief that I watched John sail to Wally and Phil.

It was clearing more and more now and I could see the shore and yacht club again. When I finally reached the pier I was so exhausted I couldn't even talk. I felt completely drained, physically and mentally.

Unfortunately, it was at this time that Georgia, Phil's wife, who was standing on the end of the pier, asked me where her husband was.

Under more alert circumstances, I would have noticed the agony written in her face, and the horrible conclusion she had drawn when I returned alone. All I could manage was a feeble gesture while struggling to get the boat safely moored. Georgia misinterpreted this as meaning her husband had been lost at sea. The anguish on her face, however, finally brought me to my senses, and I explained what had happened.

To this day the experience is still vivid in my memory and hindsight suggests a number of things I could and should have done differently—like put on our life jackets when I saw that squall coming. To a sailor, bad weather never comes as a surprise and we should have been ready.

I often recall that day, and wonder at the cool courage of Wally and Phil when they suddenly found themselves stranded in a severe squall in the middle of the Bay without life jackets, and the question of "What if ...?" still causes a knot to tighten in my stomach.

Mrs. Hemard's Hen

(An Almost True Story)

New Orleans, 1930. It was hot, and we were poor. It was my first birthday and my mom, a youngster herself, wanted it to be a memorable one. She was only seventeen. Dad was nineteen. They had been married about a year and had lived with my dad's mom until recently. Now, for the first time, they were really on their own.

Being a wife, mother and housekeeper in her own home was brand new to Mom, and she found herself wishing she had been more observant of the skills of homemaking when she had been with grandmother. But it seemed that such skills interested most young girls only when they became necessary. To celebrate my birthday, Mom wanted to have a special supper for Dad that night when he came home from work. Money was scarce and so were jobs, but Dad had a job delivering Standard Coffee in a company truck with their motto written on both sides: "Rain or shine, I'm on time."

Mostly, Mom and Dad lived off of love, I guess, because Mom, being no more than a young girl, wasn't much of a cook yet. Mom was good at things that pleased her most, like dancing, playing the ukulele, and loving Dad.

She had just recently won the Charleston contest for the City of New Orleans. The contest had been held last Saturday night at the old Orpheum Theater just off Canal Street. The prize had been fifty dollars that had meant an awful lot to Mom and Dad. Dad only made twenty-five dollars a week. Mom was elated that she had won. Of course, Dad bringing his old bachelor buddies around to cheer for her didn't hurt any. But she had been the best. She knew it and so did the judges.

Trying to make ends meet, Mom had tested the color of her thumb in a tiny backyard garden of a typical New Orleans "shotgun" one-bedroom house, which they had just rented. Shotgun meant that as you came in the front door it was a "straight shot" through all the rooms to the back door.

Anyway, she had tried to plant a few things in a small backyard, enclosed by tall, green wooden fences on three sides. She had not been too successful, except for a few shallots, which she had transplanted from the levee where they grew wild. She had tried tomatoes and a little lettuce but what had managed to grow became victims of her neighbor's Rhode Island Red hen as it made flying forays across the fence, steadily depleting her meager crop until there was little or nothing left. She hardly knew her neighbor, other than her name was Mrs. Hemard, and that she was a widow with a fifteen-year-old daughter named Thelma.

Mom was fretting. The icebox and pantry were practically empty and she was even pressed for enough money to buy another block of ice to keep the milk and cream cheese cool. She wanted so much to have something nice for Dad on my first birthday. Red beans and rice were cheap but because they were cheap, they ate them nearly every day.

The windows were open and occasionally a breeze would find its way down the narrow alleys between the crowded clapboard houses and push the faded, flimsy curtains aside, bringing a breath of fresh air into the kitchen where Mom was having her lunch—a buttered piece of French bread which she would dunk into a strong cup of *café' au lait*.

Then, as if the sound had arrived with the short-lived breeze, she heard the cluck, cluck of Mrs. Hemard's chicken in her garden again.

I don't know if Mom really intended to do what she did or if fate just sort of took a hand. She grabbed the old oilcloth off the kitchen table and ran out the back door to her garden yelling "Shoo! Shoo!" and waving and shaking the tablecloth. She took the old fat hen by surprise and in its confusion it ran into a corner rather than fly back over the fence. "Git! Git, dammit git!"

Mom was young and agile and before she knew it she was on top of the hen waving the tablecloth that all at once covered the chicken that very nearly ran under it on its own. She pinned the tablecloth and the chicken to the ground and was just as surprised as the chicken that this had happened.

I guess instinct did the rest. The hen was making one hellacious noise so Mom just rolled her up in the old oilcloth, ran back into the house and closed the door. It must have been about this time, or maybe a little before, that the possibilities dawned on her—the hen was big and fat and the pantry was empty.

I won't attempt to judge what followed, whether it was right or wrong. I guess Mom might have wrestled with the morality of the situation for a moment or two, but for the most part, she was preoccupied wrestling with the hen. But then, the hen no longer looked like a hen to her, at least not a feathered one. It looked like a hen dressed, cooked and tasty from basting and seasoning.

She could already see the oilcloth cleaned and back on the table, places set, and the candle that they used when the lights went out, standing in a saucer, centered and lit. She could see a feast and a big smile on Dad's face, so happy that he was married to such a thoughtful and resourceful young wife and mother. He would not ask, of course, where the chicken had come from, or would he? She swept that thought back into a corner of her mind where she kept things she didn't like to think about, and then got down to basics.

How do you clean and cook a chicken, she wondered. She never had and could only vaguely recall what others had done. She knew the head had to come off, and now that she was committed, she proceeded with grave resolve.

Holding the hen by its legs she opened the drawer and pulled out the big butcher knife. The hen flapped its wings wildly and let loose with a loud squawk as if knowing the mission of the knife. For a few minutes it was a standoff—the hen trying to fly, while Mom held tightly to her legs.

Finally, Mom got one of the wings in her grip also, and this effectively put an end to the fowl's aeronautics. She moved to the sink and pinned the hen to the old wooden cutting board, turned and twisted the chicken until its neck was properly stretched across the board, then, whack!

Only it wasn't a good whack. There was blood spewing about the sink and instead of the loud squawking and clucking, there were only guttural, disconcerting noises emitting from the chicken. The head was still attached to the body and the body was still very much alive.

With the determination found only in a desperate woman, Mom whacked again, and this time it was a good whack. Off went the head and out spewed and splattered more blood. The one wing she had been holding got loose and assisted the other wing in spreading blood all over the sink, the floor and Mom. Outside would have been better, Mom thought briefly and belatedly. But she held on, encouraged by the vision of Dad's smiling face when he sat down by candlelight to a roasted chicken dinner, proud of her, proud of me—a beautiful happy ending—except for her conscience, which would not be stilled.

At last the chicken succumbed and Mom plopped it in the sink. Being a tidy person, and also not being too sure how to proceed from there, she thought first to clean up the mess and just briefly thought how much less mess it would have been to have had red beans and rice.

After cleaning things up, she turned her attention back to the chicken. She knew it had to be gutted and the feathers had to come off. She tried the feathers first and mostly they refused to part from the hen. Who could she ask?

There was a little grocery on the corner called Signiglio's. She had been there several times since moving to the neighborhood and had noticed dressed chickens for sale. It would be kind of embarrassing to ask but she didn't have a lot of choice.

Things were getting more complicated and she could not help but think again how much simpler beans would have been. Mustering her courage and pocketing her pride, she left the chicken in the sink and walked to Signiglio's with me riding her hip.

She didn't know how to clean the chicken and that was just the first step. She wasn't even sure how to cook it. Maybe she could even compromise and sell or swap the chicken for beans and rice and maybe even a dessert, and all the while, the guilt she had locked in the back room of her mind, persisted in banging on the door and making itself heard.

Mrs. Signiglio had just finished with a customer as Mom stepped up to the counter. Mr. Signiglio was across the aisle placing canned goods on a shelf and followed the ensuing conversation with amused interest.

"Can I help you?" Mrs. Signiglio asked.

"Well …" began Mom, not knowing quite how to start, "I've got a chicken to clean with feathers and all and I don't know how. Can you help me?"

Mrs. Signiglio smiled and asked, "Well, is it alive or dead?"

"It's dead. I just cut its head off and tried to pull some of the feathers off. I thought about cleaning it and all and cooking it, and it's important. It's my baby's first birthday and I want to have a nice supper for him and his father. Maybe I shouldn't though, because I really don't know how. Maybe I could swap or sell you the chicken for some red beans and rice or something else." She felt awkward and embarrassed, but fragmented as they were, her words conveyed her plight clearly.

Mrs. Signiglio listened to Mom with sympathetic understanding.

"What would you rather have? Red beans and rice, or roast chicken and dumplings with gravy?" She had a married daughter about the same age as

Mom, and understood. These were tough times for everybody, especially for young couples trying to get started.

"Oh, the chicken and dumplings with gravy sounds great, but I don't know how to cook that well and I'm not sure I can afford to buy very much," she said, thinking of the two dollars she had in her coin purse. She still needed to buy ice that afternoon when the wagon came around, and milk in the morning, which would leave very little to last until Dad's Saturday paycheck.

"Well, ten cents will get you enough flour for gravy and dumplings, and the rest is just preparing and cooking," encouraged Mrs. Signiglio.

The short of it was, Mrs. Signiglio took Mom under her wing and explained how to put the chicken in hot water to remove the feathers. She went into detail on how to clean and dress the chicken, how to cook it, and how to prepare the gravy and dumplings.

"What about dessert? Certainly you are going to have ice cream and cake for a birthday?" asked Mrs. Signiglio.

Mom's eyes paused briefly and studied the prices on the assortment of cakes in the bakery section and the varied flavors of ice cream advertised behind the counter. She just couldn't do it all. She would just have to manage with what she had. She did get a loaf of fresh French bread for ten cents, a dime block of butter and some garlic for five cents.

"Thank you, you've been very nice, but I believe that will be all," Mom said, a little embarrassed.

Both Mr. and Mrs. Signiglio looked at each other and watched Mom as she left the store.

Once back in her home Mom felt her spirits rising and she was confident of a fine supper for her husband and child. It was early afternoon. She should be ready by the time Dad got home.

Everything was working out fine. Soaking the chicken in hot water made it easy to remove the feathers. She followed all of Mrs. Signiglio's instructions to the letter and soon the chicken was in the oven cooking and the dumplings were prepared. She turned on the radio and picked up some "flapper" music and in growing good spirits, grabbed her ukulele and did a quick rendition of the Charleston right there in the middle of the kitchen.

Mrs. Hemard and her daughter, Thelma, had been at the Orpheum the night Mom had won the Charleston contest. They were both full of praise and Thelma had asked Mom if she would teach her how to do the Charleston sometime.

Thinking about the Hemards put a damper on Mom's joy and supper preparations. The fact still remained that the chicken she was cooking was not hers but belonged to Mrs. Hemard. Well, she had a right to protect her garden, didn't she? The rationalization helped a little but it did not cure.

Mom continued to baste the chicken and do exactly what Mrs. Signiglio had told her. The afternoon passed. It was five-thirty and Dad would be home soon. She had bathed herself and me, put on her prettiest dress, Dad's favorite perfume, and dressed me in my best baby-blue boy clothes.

The aroma of chicken and dumplings filled the house, everything was perfect … almost. She could not subdue her conscience. It was winning. It looked like it meant to ruin her day after all. She had overcome everything else, but not her conscience. Just when she should be feeling great, she became depressed.

Mom was not one to be pushed around very long, not even by a guilty conscience. She made her decision. She checked to be sure all was well in the kitchen and out the front door she went straight next door to Mrs. Hemard's with me bouncing on her hip again.

She knocked on the front door and no sooner had Mrs. Hemard opened the door than in gushed Mom's words:

"I'm sorry, Mrs. Hemard, but I have a confession to make. I'm cooking your big red hen. It's my little boy's birthday and I wanted it to be a nice day for him and his father. I could blame this on your chicken trying to devour my garden but that wouldn't be entirely true, even though I was counting on a few things from the garden for salad tonight. We're very short on money. We're tired of beans and I was weak and hardly resisted the temptation. I love my husband, I love my child, and I wanted to do something special for them. I'll pay you for your chicken, but I just don't have enough money right now. Just tell me how much and I promise I'll pay you as soon as I can. I want to enjoy that chicken with my family and I just can't do it without making amends to you. I'd do just about anything to be able to enjoy my family tonight but it looks like it's going to be up to you." Mom finished and expected the worst from Mrs. Hemard, which she felt she really deserved.

Mrs. Hemard said nothing at first. She just looked at Mom. Mom felt as though her eyes were reading her soul. Then, gradually, a smile found its way across Mrs. Hemard's face and she spoke deliberately, picking her words.

"Your husband and child are fortunate to have you. And you are fortunate to have such a tender conscience."

Mom really choked up then. "I … I'm so embarrassed and I'm so sorry, I just don't know what else to say."

"You've said it all, and very well. You don't have to say anything else. Just get back to that kitchen and do a good job for that little family of yours."

There were tears in Mom's eyes as she left Mrs. Hemard and back in her kitchen, she felt humbled but happy, and the aroma of chicken and dumplings were enhanced by a contented conscience.

When Dad finally arrived home he was overwhelmed by the meal Mom had prepared, and with an appetite from a hard day's work, he was ready to do it justice.

Just before sitting down at the table, there was a knock at the front door. It was Mrs. Hemard's daughter. Mom's eyes filled again as Thelma presented her with a beautiful bowl of salad, thick with tomatoes and cucumbers and Italian dressing. Mom thanked her, and Thelma came in just long enough to plant a kiss on my forehead, wish me a happy birthday and present me with a beautiful red and white ball wrapped in tissue with a big blue ribbon.

The remainder of the meal was just as Mom had dreamed it would be. The room was bursting with happiness and just as we were finishing, there was another knock at the door. When Mom opened it, there stood Mr. and Mrs. Signiglio—Mrs. Signiglio with a beautiful birthday cake with a single blue candle in the center, and Mr. Signiglio with a carton of Brown's Velvet strawberry ice cream.

Mom began to cry in earnest now. Dad got up to comfort her and give her a big hug. She collected herself with a little help from an understanding Mrs. Signiglio and insisted that they stay for dessert.

Then Mom's face lit up, and excusing herself for a moment, she slipped quickly next door. She returned in just a few minutes, all but dragging a reluctant but smiling Mrs. Hemard and her daughter, to join everyone for birthday cake and ice cream, and I enjoyed my first birthday more than I will ever be able to remember.

The Roadmasher

To the casual observer there would appear to be nothing unusual about the late model sedan waiting to merge with oncoming traffic at a busy intersection in the city's suburbs. Behind the wheel, a middle-aged man, neatly dressed in a conservative suit and tie, carefully studied the cars that paraded before him.

Brad Peterson was a salesman, a respected citizen of the community, and a "roadmasher".

At the moment, he blended perfectly into the typical, workday scene. Within the next thirty or so seconds, however, the right ingredients of circumstance and opportunity being present, Brad would select a choice morsel of unescorted femininity from the rotisserie of passing traffic and the chase would be on.

It was a potluck sport with Brad. If in that rationed period of time some tantalizing target didn't cross his sights, or because another car had pulled up behind him, he would scratch it as a loser and be on his way.

He was about to scratch this one when he spotted her. She was driving a red convertible with the top down, her blonde hair whipping the air with an alluring appeal that caused him to gun the accelerator in excited anticipation. A quick glance in the rearview mirror showed no cars approaching behind him. Luck was with him.

Brad slid expertly into the two-way street, just two cars behind her, catching a glimpse of her profile as she passed. She could have been straight from a Hollywood set. She was absolutely beautiful and her delicately carved chin, held high with dignity and poise, showed real class. This was his best catch in many miles, he thought.

In excited expectation, he immediately began maneuvering his car with the deft sureness characteristic of the professional roadmasher. Keenly alert, his reflexes perfectly tuned, he gauged the speed of the convertible and studied the traffic zipping by in the other lane.

There was no way of telling how soon she might turn off and he couldn't afford to be so conspicuous as to chase her all over town. Time was of the essence—he must close quickly.

Only a skilled roadmasher could have passed the two cars between him and the red convertible with so little tolerance in space and time. With a last minute whip of the wheel he barely avoided a head on collision with a yellow cab.

Like a knife into its sheath, he slid into the space behind the blonde, who carefully maintaining a speed just within the forty-five mile speed limit was totally oblivious of his maneuvering.

With lightning quick calculations Brad studied the intermittent pattern of oncoming cars—his eyes darting about in rapid reconnaissance. In a glance the rearview mirror showed the first car behind him had turned off, leaving considerable distance to the second—plenty of room. "Timing's just right." he thought cockily.

Almost taking off the back fender of a car moving in the opposite direction, Brad whipped into a passing position, determined to make use of the estimated fifteen to twenty seconds that remained before the next approaching car arrived.

He was alongside now, exactly matching her speed. He knew that she wouldn't look at him right away, a factor of female reserve, so he used these two to three seconds to double-check the car approaching him in the other lane, and the one following.

"Perfect."

Now his eyes returned anxiously to the girl and, as if in testimony to the accuracy of his calculations, she finally turned in curiosity, wondering why he had not continued to pass.

Using the distance between his car and hers to judge his position on the road, he was able to ignore the road itself and concentrate on the blonde—and this he did with unabashed boldness.

As her eyes met his in unguarded innocence, his brazen grin and penetrating gaze caused her to start in embarrassment and turn quickly away, a nervous uneasy frown on her face. He knew that in a second or two she would turn back, pride urging her to face up to him.

Brad edged his car even closer to her and from his higher conventional car he feasted on the exciting curvatures of her figure. Her full youthful bosom pressed eagerly against a form fitting, sleeveless navy blue blouse. Brad gawked in unrestrained satisfaction. What a catch, he thought admiringly.

Finally, with a sudden indignant twist of her delicate neck, she faced him, her eyes fierce and determined to turn his greedy, ravishing gaze. This he had also expected, and just a moment before, a quick glance ahead promised him at least fifteen seconds before it would be necessary to vacate the left lane.

His eyes met her fury with a steady, penetrating gaze that boldly searched her body and stripped her of modesty. Her will to resist weakened, her face flushed, and her eyes returned again to the road.

Elated by his success, Brad was still helping himself to heaping eyefuls, when she unexpectedly turned again and greeted him with a strangely inviting smile. Its "come-hither-ness" enchanted him. He was mesmerized by the nearness of her beauty and bewitched by her smile.

Somewhere in the dim distance a vague warning sounded, perhaps it was the faint suggestion of something hidden behind that smile, something cold, something ...

The sound of the impact was heard a mile away as the late model sedan wrapped itself like so much tinfoil, around the heavy chassis of the dump truck.

The truck, which had been preceding the convertible by several car lengths, had unexpectedly braked and was turning left, its thick, heavy body, a virtual wall of steel across the lane in which Brad had been traveling.

Worlds Apart

Reega dutifully ascended the steep, sandy slope, her head lowered to avoid the searing rays of the sun, while myriad silicon eyes glared at her from the burning sands. The day had been spent foraging for the Queen and as usual they had returned fewer in number. Yesterday it had been Kan, one of the hellish quadrupeds whose random destruction often wreaked havoc on their civilization.

Today they had been caught unaware when the Flarks, their giant wings casting broad swift shadows across the land, swooped down from the sky. It happened so suddenly it was impossible for all to find shelter in time and several had been lost. Three of the royal cows, which had strayed from the city, had also been devoured.

One never knew what terror the next day would bring, for many plagued the kingdom. Even nature itself, when angered, loosed gigantic storms that deformed the face of the land.

Reega's existence was, in fact, slavery and a fact she was powerless to change. Society had precipitated into three castes: royalty, the military and the working class. Royalty consisted of the Queen, a number of kings and certain individuals who by virtue of their various abilities were spared a life among the workers.

The military comprised the strongest from all three classes and was organized like minutemen, each performing normal duties until an emergency arose.

The workers were composed almost entirely of those females incapable of reproducing, and it was their backs that carried the workload of the kingdom.

Though this oppressive environment should have constituted the conditions for a worker revolution, there existed to the contrary a blind, instinctive acceptance of their fate.

Not one female worker appeared concerned, however, about their rutted life style or the inability to achieve the fulfillment of their sex of which nature had apparently deprived them. Instead, there persisted a spirit of acquiescence and total allegiance to the Queen and the community. They were born workers and would die workers each with their own work to do, toiling throughout the day for the common good of all.

It was as if time and evolution had robbed them of will. Individuality, dignity and emotion, if they had ever existed, lay dormant through the eons. Their society was highly organized and efficient, nevertheless, particularly with regard to sex and propagation. The virile males were kings and enjoyed a life of unprecedented leisure, their only duty being to mate. All newborn were kept under the direct supervision of the Queen, who was assisted by royal nurses until the young were old enough to join their respective classes.

Reega continued to the summit with the others. There a crater-like opening descended into a black chasm. A maze of tunneled streets wound their way into the depths of the planet, which the sun tried in vain to explore.

In a world where the savage struggle for survival had reduced the dignity of life to near non-existence, they had come to seek refuge underground. Their city had only one entrance, and from its vantage point high above the surrounding land, they could effectively guard against surprise attacks by their enemies.

Just as Reega was approaching the dark opening she was pushed aside by the soldiers standing guard and a low murmur about her rose to an excited clamor.

Her Highness was coming!

From the obscure murkiness below and into the bright daylight she came, accompanied by Grarg, her favorite king. She was surrounded by an entourage of guards, members of court, military officials and many technical advisors, including Lar, her assistant in matters of state, Kerg, the royal engineer, and Makor, Chief General of the military. Kerg seemed to have the attention of everyone as he pointed out proposed plans for enlarging the city.

Then unexpectedly one of the soldiers leaped forward and pointed excitedly to the distant horizon. A few quick orders were given by Makor and her majesty was escorted to the protection of the city below along with the workers and other non-combatants.

Commands were rapidly executed and in a surprisingly short time the workers had been crowded into the city below and a cordon of soldiers had been deployed in defense.

In the distance a group of workers were in full retreat toward the city. At first the cause for their flight could not be determined. Then the thin line of yet unidentified pursuers became silhouetted against the horizon.

As the fleeing workers reached the city, the soldiers parted ranks, allowing them to pass, and as the last of the workers arrived, the fears of the populace were confirmed. It was the Red Hordes!

With frightful speed the alien force closed the distance to the city, their intention to attack apparent. Her majesty's army stiffened with anticipation for they were well acquainted with the notorious ferocity of the Reds and knew that a hard battle was imminent.

Now they could be clearly seen approaching in waves, and the soldiers on the outskirts of the defensive perimeter braced themselves for the initial blow.

With the ruthlessness of wild animals, the first of the powerful attackers pounced on the defenders, and the bitter struggle began. Time after time the hordes assaulted, and though the Queen's soldiers staggered under the onslaught, their lines did not break.

Unnoticed by either group, the land had begun to darken prematurely, and the wind rose steadily to a deafening roar, and great blinding bolts stabbed at the field of battle as though another mighty army had joined the conflict.

Then the very heavens were ripped asunder and a deluge descended on its victims. Like leaden bombs, huge globules pounded the planet and its inhabitants, striking the confused combatants to the ground.

Soon the land was an angry sea of mud. The Reds and the Queen's army, still locked in the throes of battle, struggled to remain above its surface while the dead and wounded sank helplessly beneath the smothering muck.

As the furious waters began to rise, the royal army determinedly held their ground, forcing many of the enemy to be overtaken by huge lashing waves, which, like the claws of some amorphous monster, reached out for its defenseless prey.

Frantically, the Red soldiers tried to penetrate the stubborn lines of their adversaries in an effort to escape the terrifying sea, but the city's defenders fought valiantly, and it was only a matter of time before the last of the attackers had either fallen in combat or been whisked to a watery grave by the rampaging storm.

Though the threat of the enemy had been removed, the flood continued to rise steadily, and just as the turbulent waters began to plunge over the rim of the crater, threatening to inundate the city and its dwellers, the winds began to lessen and the seas to subside.

Reega, together with hundreds of others, had been crowded into the dark passageways beneath the ground. Though normally resigned to obedience, the tension of the siege coupled with the menace of the raging floodwaters began to tell on the masses of workers.

As the waters began cascading to the city below, panic gripped their hearts, and the dungeon-like confines became a living quagmire of frightened beings.

Reega was among a large group who, fearful for their lives, overpowered the guards in an effort to reach the sanctuary of high ground and accidentally they burst into the royal chambers.

In the confusion Reega found herself only a few paces from Grarg the Queen's favorite king. As their eyes met a strange thing happened. Something stirred deep inside Reega, a yearning that time and evolution had presumably extinguished. She moved closer to him, awkwardly, yet under a compulsion she could not resist.

Reega was oblivious of the others and of the struggle taking place as the guards tried to clear the chambers. She had not even noticed the Queen, who perceiving her attentions to Grarg, was also overcome by an alien feeling. She didn't know why but she knew she must destroy this worker whose body now touched that of Grarg.

Reega was ruthlessly returned to reality as the Queen, driven by her first taste of jealousy, found herself determinedly trying to strangle the life out of one of her subjects, and just as intently Reega found herself trying to do the same to her Queen.

Reega was overpowering the Queen when all at once they both stood as still as marble and listened …

Something was wrong … the Queen and Reega no longer seemed concerned about each other. It appeared as though some more horrible dread had suddenly diminished their quarrel. An ominous silence fell upon guards and workers alike.

It was hardly perceptible at first just a slight tremor. Then slowly it grew … louder and louder! The entire city began to tremble and quake violently, and in the next moment …

The bright red of the hunter's jacket and shiny rusty coat of his Irish setter presented a striking contrast against the pale yellow-brown of the open field. The day was beautiful and an early afternoon thunderstorm had left the air fresh and clean.

Following closely behind his anxious pointer, the hunter suddenly stopped and glanced down, experiencing briefly a sensation of guilt. Then brushing the incident from his mind continued on his way leaving behind the crushed remains of an ordinary anthill.

White Squall

(Based on a True Story)

The soporific warmth of the October sun blended lazily with the cool autumn air as a gentle southerly breeze caressed the broad back of the bay. Immense billowing clouds burst against the deep blue sky like silent explosions in white and cast their abstract images in vague distorted reflections on the undulating sea.

The smell of mullet hiding beneath a shiny slick mixed with the fresh salt sea air, while above, a lone gull squawked in lazy circles, dipping occasionally to scoop an unsuspecting minnow from nature's gigantic bowl. Long low waves rolled evenly toward the thin line of the distant shore, there to whisper to the crystalline white sands strange tales of the sea.

Intoxicated by the nectar of the elements, the twenty-one foot sloop yawed drunkenly downwind, her large white mainsail presenting a striking contrast against the blue of the sky as it reached out, majestically commanding the invisible strength of the wind to its bidding.

Sprawled inside the cockpit, one leg draped casually over the coaming and the other stretched luxuriously along the floorboards, I nestled the tiller loosely in my armpit, struggling not too successfully against an overwhelming desire to doze.

I managed to open an eye just in time to catch a mischievous telltale moving sneakily to the lee and an unexpected jibe. Carefully nurturing the delightful mood, I altered course to windward and exercising a remarkable conservation of effort allowed my eye to remain open just long enough to see the wayward tell-tale return to its proper position while the glaring white of the sun scolded me for gazing in its direction.

On one such occasion of nautical alertness, I drowsily considered an elongated cumulus cloud lying low in the northeast. Somehow its image had managed to squeeze into my subconscious, for observing it again sometime later, I noted it had grown considerably. Still resisting any activity that would disrupt my present reverie, I absently dismissed its gray-blue color. Whatever trace of warning that may have arisen quickly yielded to the peaceful reassurance of the warm sunlight and soft breezes that persisted in the bay.

I continued on a reach across the bay, my mainsail eclipsing a large portion of the sky, when a sound reached my ears. It was so vague that my thoughts foggily debated awhile before arriving at an agreed conclusion.

Thunder.

Running the yacht slightly upwind, the mainsail moved across the sky like the curtain of a colossal stage, revealing the villain of a drama about to unfold. If it had not been in the same location and still possessing the familiar elongated shape, I would never have recognized it to be the same cloud I had so sleepily observed such a short time ago. Like Aladdin's genie it had grown into an awesome, slate-colored mass. There was no mistaking the characteristic shape and build-up.

Squall!

Rebuking myself for such a negligent appraisal of the deceptive cloud, I noted that it fell dark and menacing to the horizon. Realizing that the safety of the harbor lay some five miles behind me and upwind, I immediately tacked and brought the boat on the wind and began the long beat back, leaving the squall to my stern. Blinded by the sun, which shimmered on the water like molten silver, my eyes painfully swept the shore in search of the harbor.

The sky and the land before me basked in sunny tranquility and seemed to deny the cause of my anxiety, but one glance over my shoulder, however, more than justified my concern.

Behind me, on the far side of the bay, the squall moved across the forest and shore and out over the water, its shadow causing the bright green of the pines to turn a dull gray as if seared by an invisible fire. It had mushroomed across the entire northeastern sky and its lead clouds, like feathery fingers, were pointing the way.

A black canopy was being drawn over the world, as dark billowy swirls raced furiously over the bay. Accented against the dark background, a long, low, dusty-white cloud curled tightly just above the water forming the leading edge of the squall.

Turning again to trim the yacht, I was captivated by the contrast. It was like being between two worlds: one, serene and peaceful before me was drenched in sunlight, while behind me the other, angry and malevolent, was obscured in menacing shadow.

Though I realized the imminent danger, I could not help but marvel at such a raw spectacle of nature. I thrilled as God's awesome power became manifest, belittling all else by its presence. I felt a sudden careless disdain for fear and gazed unafraid at the stark reality of creation. At that moment a jagged bolt of lightning split the heavens like a giant blinding fissure, and the brilliant flash had not yet left the sky when the whole bay was rocked by thunder, like the kettle drums of a thousand symphony orchestras sounding together in one grand finale.

Unimpressed by the sky's frightening exhibition, the waves remained unaffected in form but a noticeable change in color was taking place. Like a chameleon, the water was rapidly throwing off the light blue of the sky for an ominous dark green.

Still hopeful that I might reach the harbor in time, I alternately watched the telltale and studied the shore over which the squall was passing, looking for the first signs of surface winds on the water. The telltale had already swung to the east as the wind hauled toward the storm.

I was sailing on a broad reach now with the boom gliding gracefully over the water and though it had changed direction, the wind showed no increase in intensity. Finally, the wind hauled dead astern, coming from the direction of the squall. Though it appeared the emerald green water could grow no darker, a thin band of still deeper green appeared suddenly along a considerable stretch of water close to shore, indicating the arrival of surface winds. I watched as they spread and raced out into the bay, and like a magic dye, the water now changed from dark green to deep blue.

I was still about three miles from the harbor but I thought that it was not yet necessary to lower the sails. I watched the dark blue agitation as it textured the water and moved closer. There was no sign of white caps yet and I decided to continue sailing. Perhaps I could use the head winds to make better time to the harbor before the main body of the squall struck.

As the first cat's paws scampered wildly across the water toward the yacht, I eased into the wind and luffed the mainsail in anticipation.

Like a giant invisible fist, the first gust of wind sank deep into the belly of the mainsail. The boat heeled, staggered by the blow, while the sails popped in startled excitement. Like a frightened yearling, the yacht froze for an instant, then leaped forward straining at the sheets, her white sails whipping the air.

The boat was moving swiftly now, the water churning beneath her bow. Hiked out over the windward side to offset a pronounced heel, I was for the moment satisfied that I could weather the present situation and pointed again for the harbor.

My confidence was short-lived, however, as I looked back towards the brownish-black cloud mass that had just moved out over the bay. The water had turned greenish-brown and white caps were becoming abundant. The waves, fed by the strengthening wind, were growing to a disconcerting size, and the boat heeled and rocked across their backs.

Then I saw what I had most feared. A vast, white, frothy sheet of foam was sweeping out from shore as a sudden increase in the intensity of the wind began lifting the foam off the whitecaps and spraying it across the water.

White squall!

The spectacle was indeed a performance of nature to be appreciated, but at the time, however, I indulged in only the briefest admiration. For at first sight of the immense sheet of white bearing down on me I threw the yacht into the wind, let go the sheets and cast the anchor, securing the line to the bow cleat as well as the foot of the mast.

Loosening the halyards I waited for the yacht to draw tight on the anchor line and lay into the wind, which would swing the boom and mainsail over the boat and into position to be lowered. The deep, hollow spanking of the mainsail and the higher pitched, faster whipping of the jib competed with the increasing howl of the wind through the shrouds.

I had not quite lowered the mainsail when a sudden gush of wind against the sails caused the boat to lay on its side and it was all I could do to hold on to the mast. The bow was rising high into the air on the crest of each wave, straining against the anchor line like a wild stallion roped for the first time. Then she would plummet and slam into the following trough with an impact that vibrated through the boat.

It seemed impossible to pull the sail over the cockpit and as it filled momentarily, the boat heeled on its side again and began to ship water. It was then I decided to just let the sails fall, and in the next instant they lay half in the cockpit and half submerged in the turbulent sea. Several times I was thrown into the cockpit and once nearly out of the boat while trying to retrieve the mainsail from the water.

All at once large drops of cold rain driven almost horizontally across the water began pelting and stinging my body. I had just managed to drag the last of the mainsail into the boat and lash it and the jib securely when it seemed the very heavens fell in an icy deluge.

There was nothing more I could do now except wait. Wrapping myself with part of the mainsail I began to shiver and futilely tried to wipe the blinding rain from my eyes. It seemed as though there was no end to the rain and wind, and the waves relentlessly pounded and washed over the boat until the cockpit was so full the water covered the floorboards.

It was as if some unseen power had suddenly commanded the squall to subside, for the wind and rain seemed at once to lessen, and what had been huge ragged waves gradually became smooth rolling swells with a thin speckle of rain dotting their surface.

Above, the clouds still raced low and furious but broken and formless like freshly stirred buttermilk, and the whole bay grew brighter as the sun strained to pierce the thinning overcast.

I had begun to bail, the activity bringing a little warmth back to my body, but not yet enough to still my chattering teeth and shuddering muscles. Then the welcome warmth of the sun finally punctured the grayish clouds above and, like the beams of powerful searchlights, spotlighted large bright areas of shimmering water.

Gaping holes of brilliant blue sky began to appear and the wind had all but stopped, causing the water to smooth and mirror the clouds above. Finally, the sky overhead was completely blue and the gray-blue of the storm retreated to the distant horizon.

I finished bailing the bilge and hauled up the sails again, their wet, shiny surface glistening in the warm sun. A gentle southerly breeze had returned and began to emboss the smooth water with tiny ripples that continued to join and grow. I hauled in the anchor and trimmed the sails. Gradually, the bow began softly to stir the water.

Exhausted, I sprawled in the cockpit, one leg draped casually over the coaming and the other stretched luxuriously along the floorboards, while above a lone gull squawked in lazy circles.

The Fantastic Muse

It was the last of May, 1949, and the last class of the year was approaching its end. A small group of students gathered closely about the steady blue flame of a Bunsen burner, their faces contorted in an all too obvious pretense of interest. In their midst rose the towering, lanky form of Michael Dunn, Assistant Professor of Chemistry at Kentwood College.

As the students watched, he picked up a solid glass rod with a short sliver of platinum wire extending from one end. Expertly he dipped the wire into a partially filled beaker, extracted it being careful not to lose the tiny droplet that had adhered to the tip. He thrust the droplet into the cone of the flame. Instantly, a beautiful scarlet glow appeared, then quickly died, as the platinum wire grew white-hot.

"There you have it," he said. "A positive flame test for the element strontium. Are there any questions?" It appeared for a moment that one student was about to ask a question, but the sudden cold stares of his classmates caused him to reconsider.

Pretending to be unaware of the unanimous censure, Professor Dunn turned to the young man who had started to raise his hand. "You had a question, Mr. Thompson?"

"Oh no, no sir. I was just going to remark how ah … how striking the color had been," replied the young man, his eyes apologetically seeking the forgiveness of his classmates for nearly having prolonged the class.

The professor glanced at the round, white face of the clock that stared down from the wall in wide-eyed anticipation. Only fifteen minutes and the last class would end.

"Well, are there questions on any of our other experiments?" He asked, probing their defenses.

Mute silence.

There was a noticeable movement as the class slid in unison to the edge of their seats anticipating an early dismissal.

"If not, then I suppose we still have time for a short review," he said, managing not to smile at their comic impatience. Terrible grimaces of pained disappointment flashed across the faces before him accompanied by a number of low moans. Unable to contain himself any longer, Mike chuckled. "O.K., gang, class dismissed. And have a good vacation."

One might have found it difficult to believe that the boisterous, carefree crowd of budding humanity that surged in one movement through the doors of the lab into the hallway and out onto the campus would one day bloom into the intelligentsia of our country.

Mike walked over to his desk and sat down. Absently, he considered the empty room and vacant stools. How many young people, he wondered, had passed through here with their dreams of the future.

It had only been three years since he had been a student here, and as his eyes fell on his old lab locker, his thoughts began to drift along the tender river of reminiscence.

They settled, finally, on his last year of high school. He had been undecided about his future and what he would study in college. He had considered Law and Pharmacy before deciding on Chemistry and the teaching profession.

He had even considered journalism. In fact, as he thought about it now, it had been creative writing that had most appealed to him, but he had pushed that possibility aside as too impractical, too much of a gamble, and had gone on to earn his Bachelor of Science, and later, his Masters Degree.

The desire to write had remained, however. Though buried beneath the stringent demands of a teaching career and further studies, he had still hoped to try his hand someday.

Why not now? He thought. He had made no plans as yet for the vacation months other than a few hours of tutoring a week to maintain a little income during the summer. Why not? He would simply postpone beginning work on his doctorate until fall. After all, he was only twenty-five. What was the hurry? Besides, it would be the closest thing to a vacation in years.

Actually, there was more to his desire to write than he cared to admit. In his choice to teach, he had selected what he considered security, a livelihood that he could rely on in later years, but as is inherent in most of us, there persisted the desire to achieve something personally creative, something that would lift him above the norm of mediocrity.

It wasn't that he was dissatisfied with teaching. He really enjoyed working with his students. But he relished the idea of being an author. Writing seemed to lend a certain dignity to one's existence, a unique independence that could be found in few other endeavors.

He was still dreamily considering the prospects of becoming a successful writer when a soft feminine voice interrupted his reverie.

"Hello, Professor, remember me, your date for lunch? Or can't you bear to part with the pleasant aromas of your scientific pursuits?" teased a beautiful young blonde of attractive proportions, mockingly holding her nose.

"Hi, Terry," answered Mike, glancing quickly at his watch. "I'm sorry, I didn't realize the time …"

"My, but you were in deep thought. I didn't know you were given to such prolonged periods of meditation," she said, still teasing.

"Guess I got carried away," he conceded.

"I wish I could carry you away like that," she said, moving close to him, her hands lightly resting on his shoulders. A fragrance of violets suddenly replaced the sour odor of chemicals and he yielded to a desire to fill his nostrils with its sweetness.

"Terry, you are so beautiful. I …"

She moved still closer and the soft warmth of her body lightly pressed against him. He closed his eyes and felt the pleasant moisture of her lips gently touch his own. Then, as she moved slightly back, his eyes opened and looked into the sparkling blue of her own. Whatever he had been about to say vanished from his mind and all that remained was a dumbstruck adoration of this beautiful girl.

Embarrassed that he should still be so affected by her touch, he cleared his throat and began clumsily sliding some papers into his briefcase.

Cocking her head to one side so their eyes would meet again, Terry smiled. "Then you are still mine, aren't you? And just as shy as ever. But don't you ever change. I love you for that. But what were you in such deep thought about when I came in?"

Holding her small hands in his own, he planted a quick kiss on the dainty nose before him. "What do you say I tell you all about it over lunch at Jake's" he suggested, resisting an impulse to scoop her into his arms and return her kiss a hundredfold. Kentwood was generally broad-minded about such things, he thought, but after all, she was a dean's daughter.

Mike had met Terry Andrews at a school dance shortly after her father, Dr. Andrews, had accepted the position as Dean of the English Department.

At that time he had been diligently applying himself toward his master's degree and had become somewhat of a bookworm, complete with horn-rimmed spectacles. This studiousness, plus a natural shyness, had caused him to be rather withdrawn.

It had been his old chemistry professor, Dr. Williams, who had advised him that it was just as important to develop socially as academically. This was necessary, he said, particularly in the teaching profession. No one likes a stick-in-the-mud teacher.

His words had their intended effect. Mike had not realized how narrow his interests had grown, and began frequenting campus social events and the various school activities such as sports, dances, concerts, etc. It was while attending these functions that he began to notice a certain girl and each time he saw her he experienced something like a thrill, a longing …

The thought of actually trying to meet her rather unnerved him. She seemed far out of his reach, full of life and always surrounded by friends. In spite of this, he began to inquire about her, trying to attract as little attention as possible in doing so. Adding even more to the aura that seemed to surround her, he discovered she was an English graduate student and that her father was Dean Andrews, head of the English department. He also found out that she worked part time in the University library where he found himself spending more and more time "researching."

Mike found himself beginning to watch for her wherever he went and would walk out of his way in order to "accidentally" intercept her. They had begun to recognize each other on campus, and were now greeting one another with "Hi," a major breakthrough as far as Mike was concerned.

At a dance he saw her again. He would probably never have had the courage to introduce himself to such a vivacious, attractive girl on his own. He had been talking to Dr. Williams when the new dean of English and his daughter, Terry, joined them and introductions followed.

He had felt terribly stupid, not being able to think of a thing to say, and what made it even more embarrassing, neither could he remove his eyes from the girl who stood before him.

To make things worse, Dr. Williams, noting Mike's stricken state, had decided to play cupid and had led Dean Andrews to another group, leaving him alone with Terry.

"If you are afraid to talk to me, perhaps we could dance." Her words jolted him and he started to retort defensively but the warm sincerity of her smile completely disarmed him. All at once he was at ease and found his voice.

"Thank you," he said, "It's been a long time, but I'll try."

As he felt the warm softness of her body against his own, he was at once embarrassed and excited and his heart beat so hard that he thought she would surely feel it. Somehow, his feet had managed to move, and still more remarkable, they had remained on their own part of the floor.

Once she leaned her head back so that only inches separated their faces and he was aware of the fragrance of violets. Briefly, her smile lessened and her eyes regarded him intently. The intimacy of her gaze caused his face to grow suddenly warm.

"I'm sorry," she said, seeing his discomfort, and returned her head gently to his shoulder.

The spell was broken momentarily as the orchestra began playing a lively piece. Mike stopped, reluctantly removing his arm from around her slender waist.

"I'm sorry, but I'm afraid that's a little fast for me," he apologized, feeling guilty. "Maybe you would like to meet some of the other boys," he offered by way of atonement. Immediately, however, he regretted his suggestion.

There was only the slightest trace of disappointment in her expression, but Mike noticed it.

"Truthfully," he braved, "the last thing in the world I want to do right now is to share you with someone else."

The ease with which the words had come surprised him and he was about to apologize for being so forward when he noticed she was looking at him again with that same penetrating gaze that before had caused him to blush. This time, however, he held her eyes steadily with his own, making no effort to conceal what he knew they would tell her.

After the dance, Mike was walking Terry home across the campus. The autumn night was cool and without thinking he reached for her hand, and wondered if he should have. His doubts were relieved, however, when she gently accepted his in her own. He felt her warmth surge through his whole being. They were silent. Words would have been superfluous. Stopping in the deep shadow of a large cedar, they watched a familiar glow begin to chase away the darkness just above the horizon. Adorned only in the scarlet of her modesty, the moon peeked shyly from behind a distant mountain, hesitated a moment, then rose serenely, gracefully unveiling her radiant beauty.

As their lips parted, Mike wondered if it were too early to know … could this be love?

Mixing with the mass exodus of students, Mike and Terry made their way across the sundrenched campus, through the ivy-covered archway and into the town of Kentwood. You could almost hear the old school sigh in relief as it settled back among the shady oaks to enjoy the quiet restfulness of a summer's respite.

After finding a quiet booth at Jake's and placing their order, Mike began, "Terry, I've decided to do something I've been wanting to do for a long time. I've decided to try my hand at writing fiction. This probably comes as a surprise to you but after graduation from high school, I had almost decided to study journalism rather than chemistry. It's been in the back of my mind for a long time but the necessity to earn a secure living took priority. I don't know if I have the talent or not, but I do have the desire and I'll never know unless I try." Mike paused, waiting for her reaction.

Terry was elated. "Mike, I think that's wonderful. I believe you would be a fine writer. You're sensitive, understanding, and observant and I think these are important in a writer. I think that's great. Hmm ... Michael Dunn, author. Sounds very dignified. Will you let me help you with proofreading?

"Certainly," he said, "there's a woman behind every great man," he laughed.

Dreamily, Mike pictured himself lounging in a plush leather chair, pipe in hand, while Terry marveled at the sheer mastery of his creativity.

Mike paid the waiter and walked Terry home; the young would-be author and his devoted advocate pursuing a lofty discussion of great authors and great books.

After seeing Terry home, Mike finally turned into the walkway of an ancient looking, three-story home. It was a bulky incongruous structure with random outgrowths of dormer windows, built in the days when homes were as generous with their rooms as families were with their offspring.

It had been built before the Civil War by Mike's great grandparents, James and Martha Dunn, and had afforded ample space for their eight children. From there the names on the family tree had increased as each of the original eight Dunns had proven to be equally prolific.

Mike made no pretense, consequently, in being familiar with the virtual landslide of Dunns that had occurred during the past hundred or so years. Throughout this time the old home had always been inhabited by some member of the Dunn clan, presently by George Dunn, his father's oldest brother, and George's wife, Marie.

Shortly after graduation Mike's parents moved from Kentwood to the northern part of the state. Having been finally instated as a member of Kentwood College staff and faculty, he had decided to accept his uncle's offer to stay with him in the old home. George and Marie welcomed the idea of having a young man about the house again and Mike enjoyed their company. The majestic old building with its numerous rooms was in itself an attraction. Although he had been there several months, parts of the home still lay unexplored.

After dinner that night Mike excused himself, and went to his room on the second floor, anxious to begin his literary venture. He had decided against mentioning it to anyone other than Terry until he had at least made some kind of a beginning. Not having as yet the remotest idea of a plot in mind, he was anxious to be alone with his thoughts, to call on his latent power of imagination that, once aroused, he felt certain would provide him with a Pulitzer Prize winning story.

It was disconcerting therefore, when after being seated at his desk for the better part of an hour, he had nothing to show for his efforts except the teeth marks on his pencil.

It wasn't that ideas had not occurred to him. On several occasions he had started to touch his pencil to the virgin white paper, but each time he had stopped, suddenly critical of the immaturity or triteness of what he had been about to write.

The drawn lines of discouragement began to crease his face as he called in vain on that part of himself that yearned for expression. It seemed afraid to chance the embarrassment of failure and remained, instead, secure in its silence. If he could just coax that something that remained hidden inside him, to taste just once the sweet nectar of creative composition, it would henceforth dine insatiably on delightful metaphors, colorful adjectives and imaginative plots, replete in literary satisfaction. For a long moment, Mike just sat staring out the old dormer window into the night, his mind blank with fatigue, his pencil poised motionless over a blank sheet of paper.

Then something very unusual happened. It was a strange sensation, like falling asleep, like being in a dream, but realizing that he was dreaming, and though this realization should have constituted his awakening, it didn't. He continued to dream, aware of what was happening in the dream, yet, at the same time, conscious of his real surroundings.

They were his thoughts that began to form, clearly and confidently and yet they seemed foreign. It was his hand that began to move with bold certainty across the page, obediently recording the dictates of his mind, and yet it seemed to move with a detached independence. He grew tired and couldn't think … yet he did, clearly and distinctly. He wanted to sleep, and he did. Yet while he slept he listened to the thoughts, unfamiliar thoughts, and his hand wrote on relentlessly into the night.

As the heralding light of dawn announced the arrival of a new day, a single lighted window could be seen standing guard over the sleeping city, patiently awaiting its relief, the sun. Bashful beams of sunlight hesitated a moment at the edge of the window, apprehensive about disturbing the man asleep at his desk. Then as their numbers increased, they rushed into the room with renewed courage, recklessly splashing themselves about.

Mike winced as the inquisitive sunbeams began dancing about his face, playfully trying to pry themselves under the tightly squinted lids of his eyes. His waking thoughts stumbled groggily about unable to orient themselves in the still sleep-darkened chambers of his mind.

Finally, managing to bear the brilliance of the sun-soaked room, he opened his eyes. His first attempt to rise on his elbows was met with failure as he conceded that somehow during the night he had broken his neck. Every movement was instantly resisted by an array of aches and pains.

Eventually succeeding in gently balancing his head between an ache and a pain, he paused to consider his next move. It was then that he became aware of the profusion of papers strewn across his desk.

My God! he exclaimed to himself, as he saw page after page of longhand. His neck smarted as he momentarily forgot the crick that was there, and then began collecting the scattered writing with both hands.

Why, I must have written all night, he thought, absently arranging the papers. He stopped short—the realization so stunned him he could only gape in astonishment at the manuscript before him. It seemed transformed all at once into a thing unreal. He had not the vaguest notion what it contained.

Unable to comprehend such an absurdity, he began a slow, deliberate examination, becoming even more befuddled when the text began with an incomplete sentence on page one hundred and twenty and a rapid thumbing of the pile of paper turned up no preceding pages! Then he encountered an even stranger sensation. As he continued to read, word-by-word, sentence-by-sentence, he had no idea what the next would bring. Yet, as he read he seemed to remember having thought the ideas before, and having written the words before. But the words—some he could not recall ever using, and still more bewildering, there were others he didn't even recognize!

For a fleeting moment he was ready to disallow having written what was before him, but the unmistakable lines of his own handwriting could not be denied. In spite of his perplexity, the text fascinated him. He continued to read, enthralled, until he had finished it.

It appeared to be a historical novel, taking place during the Civil War. He marveled at the realistic portrayal of human emotions, the strength and individuality of the characters, each personality being forged by life's circumstances. Equally impressive was the attention to detail, particularly regarding the war.

He stopped—abruptly extracting himself from the mesmerizing effect of the manuscript. He had no such knowledge. Yet, he had written it! The full impact of this act caused a sudden anxiety to rise within him, and in a brief moment of panic, he pushed noisily away from the desk, and stood up staring incredulously at the manuscript. His eyes darted around the room expecting that perhaps something would suggest an answer, or maybe the reality of the room and its familiar furnishings would somehow diminish the paradox that confronted him.

Slowly his hands reached out and gathered up the white pages, grayed by closely penciled longhand. He held them between his fingers as if to reassure himself of their existence, then sat down again.

Struggling to remain calm, he tried to think, to reason. There must be an explanation. Yet the more he sought a logical answer the more convinced he became that such a thing simply could not be. His mind, unable to cope with such a contradiction, was forced to conditionally accept the impossible, to set reason aside for the moment until he could regroup the routed forces of his intellect.

"Mike? Oh, Mike? Are you up yet?" Marie Dunn was gently knocking at his door.

Hearing his aunt's voice was like waking in another world, a world simple and uncomplicated. His voice broke hoarsely in response.

"Yes, Aunt Marie, I'll be down in a minute, just tidying up a bit."

"Breakfast will be ready in about fifteen minutes, son, and we have a pretty guest to join us," she teased in sham mystery.

Terry, he thought. The warmth of her name seemed to challenge the chilling problem that had besieged him. Her very presence appeared to dispel the unpleasant, to allay his anxiety. Yet he knew that the mystery that had so rudely injected itself into his life, was no less real, no less baffling.

When Mike was halfway down the soft-carpeted stairs, the aroma of flap-jacks, fried sausage, and strong coffee assailed his nostrils and it seemed he could already taste the tangy, sweet maple syrup.

On entering the dining room, his eyes swept the room only briefly, for as they fell on the bright soft beauty of Terry, all else appeared only as a backdrop, like props of a stage designed only to enhance.

"Well, good morning, sleepy head," jibed Terry in high spirits.

"Hi," he answered, feeling he should add something. He wanted to match her mood, but the occurrence during the night had hobbled his wit. Embarrassed by his reticence, he averted his eyes, sat down and busied himself by placing a napkin on his lap.

Marie was flitting about serving, pausing periodically to refill a cup with steaming black coffee. His uncle was politely pretending an interest in the conversation while sneaking glances at the morning paper.

Terry, however, had not failed to note that something was troubling Mike and tried to cheer him. "Well, Uncle George, what do you think of your nephew's plans to become a writer?"

A quizzical expression from Marie left a cup half filled with coffee, while George's fork paused in midair with a thick juicy piece of sausage dripping at random on the tablecloth.

Mike looked up frowning with an "I wish you hadn't said that" look. The glances of the small group ricocheted in silence from one to the other, and Terry again felt obliged to speak. "Sorry, Mike, I didn't mean to … I thought you would have told them by now," and her eyes apologetically sought his.

George, sensing an awkward situation, relinquished the morning news and rose to the occasion. "Well, I'll be a monkey's uncle, what do you know about that? Come on now, let's hear about it," he urged.

What success Mike had in temporarily shelving the dilemma upstairs vanished, and the enigma of the manuscript returned to plague him. How to treat the problem now at hand escaped him completely. He managed a delaying smile as he thought of what to say.

Terry knew now that something was wrong. Still trying to make the best of her unintentional blunder, she tried again. "Sorry, Mike, forgive me." Then looking at George and Marie, "He didn't want to tell you yet and I spoiled it," she finished, sure that this would satisfy Mike's aunt and uncle, but was convinced now that something altogether different was troubling Mike.

The stimulating effect of hot coffee and Terry's sensitive concern raised Mike's spirits. His determination to find an answer was renewed. He must not arouse suspicion, however, until he had more time to think. "All right, all right. I had intended to keep this between Terry and me until I had at least made a start," then smiling added, "Just wanting to write doesn't make me a writer you know."

"Then you have started?" interrupted George. "That's why your light was on so late last night."

Again, Terry saw Mike's brow crease in uneasiness.

George continued, however, ignoring Mike's reluctance to discuss the subject. "Well, Marie," he said, as if by proclamation, "it looks like we're going to have another writer in the Dunn family."

Seeing that Mike was awkwardly exposed on a subject he was not yet ready to discuss, Marie turned to him apologetically. "Mike, you'll have to excuse that long nose of your uncle, he's been that way for thirty years and will probably be the same for another thirty." she said laughingly, with a gentle glance of rebuke toward her husband.

"Sorry, Mike," apologized his uncle on cue, "Marie's right, I had no business prying."

"George, please don't let that bother you," answered Mike, "I'm pleased that you're interested."

A puzzled look suddenly spread across his face as his uncle's earlier remark washed again to the surface of his thoughts. "Did you say another writer in the Dunn family?"

"Sure," answered his uncle, glancing quickly at his wife for permission to continue. "Don't you remember Jeffrey Dunn?"

"No, I can't say that I do, guess I missed him somehow. What about him?" he encouraged.

"Well," began his uncle, settling back in his chair and handing Marie his empty coffee cup, "Jeffrey Dunn was a very talented young writer, wrote I don't how many articles for magazines and newspapers; had a promising career ahead of him."

"Had?" joined Terry, noting Mike was more or less himself again.

"What happened?" asked Mike, impatient for his uncle to swallow his coffee.

"Yes, it was a terrible waste," George went on; relishing the interest he had stirred, "Just as the world was about to open before him he was killed at the battle of Gettysburg. He was an officer in the Confederate army, cavalry I believe."

"How old was he?" asked Terry, not noticing the strange expression twisting slowly across Mike's face.

"Twenty-nine, I believe," George answered, "and it was a real pity. That boy really had talent, an unusual gift for words. In fact I believe he had just begun writing his first novel when he was killed. Very sad, he used to live in this house, you know, used the attic upstairs for his study. It was the only place where he could find a little peace and quiet, I guess. As big as this house is, a family often must've filled it up pretty well, I imagine.

"I believe copies of some of his articles are still in the attic," continued George, "along with some old portfolios that were packed away years ago. They're in one of several old trunks with other Dunn family memorabilia. Never have got around to going through it all. Keep telling myself I will one day."

"Sounds as though it would be a really interesting thing to do," said Terry. "I'd love to see …" The expression on Mike's face caused Terry to stop.

The idea was so incredible it jolted Mike into silence, his mouth agape in astonishment.

"Mike? What's wrong? You look like you've seen a ghost," Terry queried.

"Well, I …" mumbled Mike distractedly. The thought had paralyzed his mind. Could that possibly be? The strange circumstances under which he had written the unfamiliar words, the detailed knowledge of the Civil War … and the missing beginning.

"Mike?" Terry tried to break through the trance-like expression that seemed to have frozen on Mike's face.

"Mike, are you all right?" his uncle asked, also becoming concerned by his behavior, "you're white as a sheet, son."

"I'm O.K … really. "He finally answered. Then turning to his aunt and uncle, asked if they would excuse Terry and himself. Not waiting for an answer, he turned to Terry, his eyes beseeching and tense. "Terry, will you come with me, please?"

Leaving the table, he started toward the stairs, then paused to wait for Terry, who, with eyebrows arched in question, glanced quickly at George and Marie, shrugged, then quietly followed.

Once upstairs Terry assailed Mike with questions. "What's the matter, Mike? What's wrong? Was it something I said? Why are you acting so strange? Well …? Say something, Mike," she insisted, becoming just a little more than concerned.

Finally, she stopped in the middle of the upstairs hallway and folded her arms with pretended petulance waiting for Mike to answer her.

Mike turned, walked back and took her gently by the arm. "Please, Terry, I must do it this way." Still not trusting himself, he wanted Terry to corroborate what he had concluded. Let her read it, he thought. Explain to her the circumstances under which he had written the unfamiliar words—the incomplete text. Remind her of George's reference to Jeffrey Dunn's "old portfolios", his service in the Confederate cavalry, his death ... and then see if they were both losing their minds.

Unable to resist Mike's gentle persuasion, she followed him down the hall to his room. He opened the door, walked to his desk and pulled the chair out and motioned for her to sit. Pointing to the neatly stacked manuscript, he said simply, "Read that, please." then walked to the window and stood silently staring outside.

Recognizing Mike's handwriting, Terry's eyes brightened in interest. She turned and started to say something but noting the tenseness in Mike's face, her eyes returned instead to the manuscript. As soon as she encountered the incomplete sentence, she stopped and glanced at the page number. It indicated page 121. After searching through the manuscript for some time, she finally looked up questioningly, "Mike, where is the beginning? This starts on page 121," she said, pausing, expectantly. "That's all there is, Terry. Begin reading there," said Mike, without explanation, his back still to her.

"But, Mike, that's crazy," she persisted.

"Terry ... that's where it begins, there is no more. Please read it."

The blunt manner, in which he had stated such an obvious absurdity, caused her to suddenly feel uneasy. It didn't make any sense, thought Terry to herself, and though disturbed by the strangeness of the situation, she began, nevertheless, dutifully to read.

As her interest was more and more aroused by the text of the manuscript, she ignored for the moment the problem of the missing pages, feeling certain an explanation would follow later.

Almost a half hour had passed, as Terry had read page after page, completely engrossed, when Mike turned and interrupted. "O.K., Terry, if you don't mind, I'd like you to stop now. You can finish it later if you like. Tell me what you think of it," he suggested, walking back to the table and sitting beside her, intent on her answer.

Taking a moment to organize her thoughts, Terry's eyes rested on the manuscript, finally, she looked at Mike, frowning slightly. "It's beautiful, but for some reason it disturbs me." She said thoughtfully.

"Why? What is it that disturbs you?" he asked, knowing what the answer would be.

Terry sensed that he had anticipated just such a reaction, still adding to the mystery that had begun to surround the manuscript. "Well, in addition to the missing beginning, when a person knows someone as well as I like to think I know you, it's disconcerting to suddenly discover a part of you I knew nothing about. Mike, it just doesn't sound like you. It's almost as if someone else wrote this." Her eyes returned questioningly to the manuscript.

"Someone else did," Mike stated matter-of-factly, his eyes fixed on Terry. "Terry, I didn't write that. My hand held the pencil, it wrote the words ... but those are someone else's words."

Terry felt her face twitch nervously. Her mind, rejecting what she had just heard, raced to find refuge in a possible misunderstanding. "You mean you got the idea from someone else?" she suggested, hopefully.

"No, I meant just what I said. Someone else used me to write it."

"But that's impossible," she said, becoming flustered by his persistence. Then, forcing a smile, she tried again to avoid the incredulity of his words. "You are joking, aren't you?"

"No, Terry, I am dead serious, make no question about it. I wrote that," indicating the manuscript, "but it belongs to another person ... a person who used my mind and my body to record his thoughts."

"His?" asked Terry, trying to maintain her composure and still probing for a reasonable explanation.

"Yes, *his*," he repeated firmly, and paused for a moment before adding ... "Jeffrey Dunn," he announced with finality. And then quickly, in defense, as Terry's mouth hung mutely open, "Terry, I've gone over it again and again. There is no other explanation. I don't care how ridiculous it sounds. There are detailed descriptions of places and events in that story of which I have absolutely no knowledge. There are words used that I have never heard and there is no other way to account for starting in the middle of a sentence, in the middle of a manuscript. I find it as difficult to believe as you, but what you or I believe or don't believe won't make that manuscript disappear."

"Mike, I ... I just don't know what to say," said Terry, unable to hide a worried glance at the manuscript and then at Mike. "It's all just come at me too fast. I really don't know what to think."

"You think I'm nuts, don't you?" he asked, reading the expression on her face. "Well, frankly, I can't say that I blame you. Maybe I have flipped, I don't know ... Wait a minute!" he said excitedly, "George mentioned something about still having some of Jeffrey's works, remember, in the attic? Where he used to write? I wonder ..."

"Mike, I ... I'm frightened" said Terry as she began to grasp the implication.

"Look, there's nothing wrong with me, I'm certain of that. Though what has happened appears incredible, I ... Terry, I'm a scientist, accustomed to investigating the unknown, and I mean to investigate this. Let the facts lead where they may. I'm going to check out that attic," he said, picking up the manuscript, "and this is going with me."

In spite of the unnerving circumstances, Terry felt suddenly proud of Mike, and was attracted by his strength. Mike, I'd like to go with you."

He was pleased. It was the two of them now. He felt a little like the knight going out to slay the dragon, anxious to impress his lady with his courage. A little histrionic, perhaps, but nevertheless, she made a difference. "All right, but not one word about this to anyone until we finish our research and sum up our findings."

"O.K, professor," she smiled, but remained anxious about what they might find.

They had no trouble talking George into opening the attic for them, using Mike's desire to also be a writer and his interest in other writers, especially one who was a member of the family. They had not, however, expected him to accompany them and tried to discourage him by laughingly accusing him of wanting to chaperon them.

"Are you sure his works are still in the attic," Mike asked as they climbed the small, hot stairwell.

"Well, it's been a long time, but no one else has been up here except the rats and squirrels, and unless they made a meal of it, it should all still be here," he laughed. The thought of anything happening to Jeffrey Dunn's writing caused Mike no small concern as they ascended the tall, almost vertical stairs.

There was no light where the stairs finally met the attic door and it seemed an eternity in the hot closeness of the stairwell before George fit the correct key into an antiquated lock.

"Seems to me I forgot to bring that flashlight the last time I came up here. Keep forgetting how dark it is in this attic," fretted George, as he pressed against the old door. Its eerie creaking as it opened caused Terry to slip her hand onto Mike's arm.

"Wait here a minute", George said, his voice fading as he moved into the inky darkness of the attic, mumbling to himself. "Let me see if I can remember where that light is … Let's see now, I seem to recall …"

"You all right?" Mike whispered to Terry.

"Sure," she said, squeezing his arm, "I just adore dusty dark stairs and squeaky old doors."

George banged noisily around the dark room, stumbling and bumping into unknown objects. "Ah." he said, and at the same moment a bright light filled the room.

A large, clear bulb swung back and forth at the end of a long cord hanging from the attic rafters, its pendulous motion causing the shadows of the room to come alive as they moved in unison with each arc of the bulb.

The attic was quite large and presented the raw appearance of construction with its bare studs along the wall and naked, sloping ceiling rafters laced with thick, black electrical wiring. A dry musty odor, like that of an old book, pervaded the room, coaxing the memory to recall days long since past.

The causes of George's stumbling were readily apparent, for it seemed that every square foot of floor space was cluttered with boxes, crates, lamps, discarded furniture, suitcases, trunks and old rugs. One small area, however, within the alcove of a boarded up dormer window seemed more or less orderly.

Against the window was an old desk and on both sides of the desk moving away from the window were bookshelves still randomly occupied by a number of dusty books of different sizes and colors. George had threaded his way to a large metal-strapped steamer trunk that sat against the wall just outside the alcove. After some difficulty he managed to open it.

"We call this 'devil's den' because it's always in a 'helluva' mess," he laughed. "You can run across almost anything up here except what you're looking for," he chuckled, "except for Jeffrey's stuff. We keep all of his things in this old trunk where they will be safe. They don't make 'em like this anymore."

Mike and Terry were slowly making their way toward George, distracted by the oddities around them. His last remark, however, caused them to have eyes only for the trunk and its contents. George had already opened the trunk and had begun to rummage inside when both Mike and Terry crowded around him, anxiously inspecting each item as he laid them out on the desk. Glancing behind him he was puzzled by the tense expression on both their faces.

"What's wrong with you two? You look like you expect Jeffrey himself to step out of this trunk. You're both pale as ghosts yourselves."

The guilty looks that immediately accompanied two contradictory explanations caused Terry and Mike to sigh in embarrassment and George to frown suspiciously.

"What's the matter? What are you two up to?" he queried, sensing he had uncovered some scheme.

"George, do you mind if we look at some of the hand-written portfolios? Then we will try to explain. In fact, we would both welcome your ideas about a problem we have," Mike offered soberly.

"O.K., O.K.," George surrendered. "This certainly has become a house of secrets." After continuing to sort through the trunk for a few more moments, he withdrew several dusty packs of paper, browned with age and neatly tied with old cord. One in particular was especially thick.

"That one," said Mike excitedly, "may I please see that one?"

Turning, George looked at their anxious faces, tapping it against the flat of his palm. "Sure," he said, his face still questioning their sudden intense interest in Jeffrey's works.

Mike's hands grew suddenly moist and he tried to swallow the dryness in his throat. Terry appeared to have turned to stone. Only her eyes moved darting from the manuscript to Mike, to George and back to the manuscript.

"Thanks," said Mike, as he stretched out his hand.

George handed it to him, his own face growing serious now as he saw the consternation in Mike's eyes.

Carefully, almost reluctantly, Mike reached toward Terry for his manuscript then laid the two manuscripts next to each other on the desk, his sweating hands leaving prints of perspiration on the slick, brown envelope as he removed the familiar pages written in his hand. It seemed he was all thumbs as he tried to untie the cord that bound the other.

"Let me," said George, forcing a laugh, "it's my knot."

While George removed the cord Mike wiped the palms of his hands dry against his trousers. "Thanks," he managed hoarsely and glanced quickly at Terry as if to say, well, this is it.

When he looked back the cord was free, the folder open and the pages of a beautifully penned manuscript, yellowed now by age, lay before him.

The first thing to catch his attention was the title, *Of Love and War*. George hadn't mentioned that, he thought. Then quickly, as if wanting to be done with it, he checked the numbering of the first three pages. Then he moved to the last page.

A giddy light-headedness suddenly overcame him as he glanced at the incomplete last sentence and compared it to the partial sentence that began his own manuscript. They matched perfectly!

"My God, it is!" whispered Mike. "Even to the page numbers!"

"Is what?" George asked. He had been looking over Mike's shoulder, his face perplexed, not yet comprehending what he saw. Turning, he looked expectantly at Mike, and then Terry.

"Mike", Terry said, "I think it's time we told Uncle George the whole story."

When Mike had finished, George's eyes had grown wide in disbelief. Then he compared the two manuscripts. The two incomplete sentences and the page numbers, though written a hundred years apart, fused the two manuscripts into one.

"Well, I'll be a monkey's uncle," was all George could stammer.

The three Dunns and Terry were seated council-like around the dining room table, Marie Dunn having likewise been introduced to the weird phenomenon that had occurred in their home. All of their objective analysis and investigation had gotten them no farther along in finding an explanation for what had occurred. It had merely substantiated that the impossible had happened and could not be explained.

After finally quitting the "how?" of this mysterious happening, Marie injected a new speculation of the "why?" of it all. This was not as difficult to determine and they had agreed on the answer. It was their unanimous opinion that Jeffrey Dunn, through some power not yet understood by them, had used Mike to finish his novel for the express purpose of publication, thus achieving that which his untimely death had denied him.

Since they were the only ones that were aware of Jeffrey Dunn's unfinished novel, it was decided that they would type it in its completed form and submit it for publication. It was also decided that the mystery of the two partially completed manuscripts would not be divulged, for no one would ever believe such a thing and would consider it a publicity stunt.

Only Mike initially dissented, maintaining that such an unbelievable happening should not be kept a secret, particularly from a scientific standpoint. Yet he agreed that no matter what evidence they produced in support, it would be the nature of people to be suspicious.

"Suppose someone should ask to see the original manuscript?" asked Mike, checking their plan for flaws.

"Well, if someone does," George returned, "we could simply delay, or just show them a portion of the original, avoiding the last page and the fact that the manuscript is incomplete. And, of course, we certainly can't show them your manuscript." Looking at the others and seeing there were no further questions, a broad smile rippled across his face. "Well then, I suggest we give this project top priority. I'm really curious what a publishing company will think about *Of Love and War.*"

Though the incredibility of the incident still lingered in each of their minds, it was more or less diminished by the speculative excitement of readying the manuscript for submission to a publisher; typing, proof-reading, re-typing and re-reading. The words of Jeffrey Dunn had become so familiar to them it was almost as though he was alive again, a real person living among them. Where he couldn't speak, someone spoke for him and usually in his own words.

It had been nearly a month since the typed manuscript had been mailed to a leading publisher and they waited anxiously for an answer. Suppose it didn't sell, thought Mike, what an anticlimax that would be. He was surprised to feel a certain satisfaction at that prospect. Though initially disguised as some vague, indefinable discontent, he finally recognized the feeling for what it really was—jealousy.

Mike had encountered his own anticlimax. His own desire to write had been buried beneath an avalanche of interest in Jeffrey. He could not quell the resentment he felt regarding the monopoly Jeffrey Dunn had achieved with regard to his aunt and uncle, and particularly the attentions of Terry.

It seemed that all Terry talked about was Jeffrey. She could quote whole paragraphs from his book, especially the romantic dialogue of the hero whom she had come to identify with Jeffrey.

In essence, Mike had a rival now for Terry's attention, a rival who had died over a hundred years ago. A rival who could no longer make mistakes, show anger or jealousy, whose words had been carefully sifted and chosen in his novel and were now unassailable in print, while his own were mostly extemporaneous and unedited. How could he compete with such a man?

At first Mike sulked over his problem and considered looking for a position in some remote, woman-less jungle where he could dedicate his bachelorhood to scientific research sans romance. This passed, however, and Mike emerged more determined than ever to win both Terry and success in his own right as a writer.

The light in his room began burning late into the night again. In the beginning it had been just like the first night when Jeffrey had barged in. He just sat, his mind ruminating and sorting various ideas for a plot. He preferred the freedom of fiction yet if he were going to achieve the degree of realism necessary to hold reader interest, it should be based at least in part on truth, something he had actually experienced.

After several false starts, an idea suddenly occurred to him. It was brazen. But the more he thought about it ... Mike smiled. It provided all the essential elements of a good story. If only he could do it literary justice. He beamed at the possibilities.

Once settled on the general theme and organization of his story, Mike had thrown himself completely into its composition. Though enthused with his subject and satisfied by the results he had thus far achieved, it was hard work, particularly for a beginner. He had hammered away every night except for an occasional night out with Terry, to whom he said nothing regarding his work. He was determined that her knowledge of his work would come only with its publication.

The going was slow and tedious. He was embarrassed by his lack of knowledge in grammar and had spent a number of hours studying his tattered old College English textbook. His work was nearly completed when a letter arrived from Alcorn Publishing Company. The contents were glorious!

The publisher was very interested and willing to pay an advance of ten thousand dollars toward expected royalties. There was a brief reference as to whom the check should be made payable. It could not be paid to Jeffrey and therefore would be made payable to George, who "has been legally determined to have sole rights to the story," and "since the subject of publishing rights was not mentioned in submitting the manuscript, a contract will need to be signed." And further, because the publisher was "anxious to get the novel to press, we are sending a representative to assist in expediting these matters. Sincerely ..."

"Ten thousand dollars!" The significance of that figure provoked much comment. "Why that's almost half of what I earn in a year," said Mike, as his hopes rose for the success of his own novel.

"Well, I'll be a monkey's uncle," said George, predictably, as he made immediate plans to contact his attorney to discuss the publisher's letter.

Marie and Terry were equally flabbergasted and spent most of their time answering the phone. A press release by the publisher had been sent to the local newspaper and the news had spread rapidly through the small college town. There was an incessant jingle of congratulatory calls from neighbors and friends, and Greg Martin, editor of the local paper, gave a front page billing complete with photographs.

Two days later a Mr. Alex Rhodes arrived from the publishing company, a contract was signed, and George accepted a check for ten thousand dollars.

George then decided that the money would be divided, half to Marie and himself and half to Mike and Terry, because all had equally shared in the enterprise of preparing Jeffrey's manuscript for publication. Mike had objected, saying that was too generous of George. But George was insistent, stating that Jeffrey had made Mike a partner by using him to complete his work and that he was certain that Jeffrey would have wanted it that way.

Only once was the subject of the original manuscript mentioned, and this was by Greg Martin, who, interviewing the family, expressed a desire to see such a valuable heirloom.

"Perhaps later," replied George, not too subtly avoiding the newspaperman's request, and instead, changed the subject to mention Mike's recent interest in writing.

Unable to determine why George had intentionally dodged his request, Greg had dropped the subject, but suspiciously eyed George and Mike and made a mental note to look deeper into the matter later. Annoyed by this, however, he responded somewhat unkindly to George's reference to Mike.

"Trying to climb on the family bandwagon, eh?" He managed a little false laugh to dilute what would otherwise have been a rather insulting remark.

With Greg it wasn't anything personal, it was just that his business was news, and in his years in the field he had developed a nose for intrigue, and something was definitely amiss here somewhere. And though Greg had not asked again to see the manuscript, George knew he had become suspicious and that they had not heard the last from him on that subject.

Mike had flushed at Greg Martin's "bandwagon" insinuation but was pleased that his suspicion had been aroused. It fit perfectly with his plan—a little premature, perhaps, but with a little luck he could turn that suspicion to his advantage.

Excited by the possibilities, Mike worked late the next few weeks and finished his novel. Then laboring over his typewriter, he set his manuscript in the proper format for submission to a publisher. Finally, he placed it in the mail to a competitor publisher of Alcorn, feeling that perhaps it would appear rather "band-wagonish" to send it to Alcorn on top of his cousin's success.

Mike was satisfied. Not that he was overly optimistic about his book being published; it was difficult to judge his own work. When he tried, his mind was a jumble of discarded sentences, scratched-out words and phrases, changed punctuation, and last minute insertions and deletions. It was only when he had read the final typed copy that lacked these pockmarked changes of the original that he was finally pleased. It would be classified as a fantasy, perhaps a little too fantastic, he thought, chuckling at the prospect, but it did possess realism and good detail. Mike smiled to himself.

It has been almost a year, Mike thought, yet he still tingled with excited satisfaction, right down to the tip of his autographing finger, each time a copy of his book was presented to him by an admirer.

While in the library researching his second novel, a young coed had approached him with a copy of his book in hand. He smiled magnanimously and opening it penned his signature with such care that one might suspect it was to be glassed-encased for posterity. He glanced briefly at the synopsis inside the shiny new cover. It had been that synopsis that had caused such a controversy.

It had provided the publicity to spark the sale of over one hundred thousand copies, winning him recognition worldwide. It had resulted in two offers for film rights, induced numerous magazines to solicit articles from him on creative writing. And thanks to a hound of a news editor, to whom Mike had discreetly led to a scoop, a fiery debate had been ignited in medical and literary circles producing the thorough investigation Mike had desired.

Yes, many wonderful things had happened in the past year, and the most wonderful of all, of course, had been his marriage to Terry, thought Mike, as he returned the autographed book to the coed.

All because of a book, a book whose plot had become as controversial as "The Lady or the Tiger."

The story had told of a young man, exceedingly desirous to become a writer, whose mind and body had been suddenly occupied by a deceased cousin in order to finish a book begun over a hundred years ago during the Civil War.

At first the publisher of Mike's book had misgivings about the fanciful plot, until, however, they became aware of a book published by a competitor company. It had been written by one Jeffrey Dunn who had died in the Civil War. It was entitled *Of Love and War*.

Then a sudden keen interest had developed in the book written by an obscure young author named Michael Dunn, who just happened to be the distant cousin of Jeffrey Dunn. The title of the new book—*The Fantastic Muse.*

Katrina, a Family Experience
(Based on a True Story)

"Here comes another one! Hang on, honey!" Ann and I both looked up to see an 8 to 10 foot muddy wave bearing down on us loaded with debris from homes and other buildings being swept away by wind and water from hurricane Katrina. We both held tightly to a multiple trunk crepe myrtle tree, my arms reaching around Ann to the tree to be sure if she lost her grip I could stop her from being swept away. As the wave rolled over us we were inundated and the force of the wave nearly tore us loose from the tree and I felt my shoes and socks sucked off my feet. We emerged from the trough of the wave gasping for breath. A short while later, maybe 15 or so seconds, another wave hit us and as the waves continued we found it more and more difficult to hold on. Ann swallowed some of the dirty, salty water and was choking. I cautioned her to take a deep breath before each wave and blow a little of the air out of her mouth when she went under to avoid swallowing water. The wind was howling so much I didn't know if she heard me or not.

During the short time between waves I felt like this could not be happening to us. How in the world did we manage to find ourselves in such a terrible predicament? Just yesterday our world was relatively normal. Though we were aware of Katrina since it had reached the mid-Atlantic, we were not overly concerned. We had been in hurricanes before, including the '47, Betsy and a few lesser storms. Then came Camille which heavily damaged Bay St. Louis, Waveland, and the entire Mississippi Gulf Coast. As Katrina drew nearer we began to go through our routine of preparations and we felt we were better prepared than we had been in previous hurricanes. We were well stocked with water and food (including dog food for Peanut, our yellow lab), flashlights and batteries, duct tape (to include pieces of cardboard to tape to broken windows) and two battery-operated radios. We had secured all outside objects that could be turned into missiles to damage the home.

Our home, which had belonged to Ann's parents, had been through Camille and other than some fairly major tree loss it had survived with little damage. The home was about a half block from the beach of the Bay of St. Louis and the waters from the Gulf had risen about eighteen inches up the outside walls. The building was on a slab with terrazzo floors and had three doors leading outside. Water had seeped through these doors allowing about eight inches of water to enter the building.

When Katrina entered the Gulf and it became a definite possibility that the Mississippi Gulf Coast and New Orleans would be likely targets, the TV began warning that people in low lying areas (flood zone areas) should evacuate. Even though the weather experts warned that this hurricane was extremely dangerous and that the water surge could reach thirty feet, I thought this to be somewhat of an exaggeration. Similar predictions had been forecast with Camille (twenty to twenty-five feet) and our home had survived. I reasoned that with the concrete car and train bridges between us and the Gulf to act as a buffer and all the tributaries to the Bay to absorb this surge we would be safe, especially if we stayed with the home and duct taped the doors.

Sunday night before the storm the wind began to increase and we could hear sizeable tree limbs falling on the roof. By morning more and larger limbs were falling. Our sons, Bishop and Matt, arrived and strongly advised us to evacuate. I still questioned the need to do this. In my mind, we were prepared, and in staying we could protect our home and its precious contents and memories, the accumulation of fifty-three years of a wonderful marriage. A man will do a lot to save his home.

Our daughter, Kathleen (Toppy), called and asked if she and her husband, Tommy, could join us with their two dogs, Odie and Dumplin. I said okay and thought it would be good to have extra hands should they be needed.

As the morning wore on the wind increased even more and I noticed that water had begun to rise on the street in front of our house. I should mention here that in Camille the winds had been clocked at 220mph and according to the news on the radio, Katrina's winds were at 165mph gusting to 200mph. plus. I felt somewhat reassured since the two hurricanes appeared to be similar.

Also, as the water began creeping well up into our yard, Toppy asked me if I thought we were in any danger. Tommy was apparently becoming concerned and thought they should leave and go to Stennis Space Center which was well above sea level. I replied to Toppy and said no, I didn't think we were in danger (again comparing this to Camille) and I mentioned that I had heard that the bridges on highway 607 to Stennis were already under water.

From then on things began to look increasingly worse. Larger limbs were falling and some trees were beginning to break in half or were being uprooted and the house which normally muted sounds from outside began to give evidence of the calamity occurring. Bishop said later that he had noticed that the bedroom wall, facing the wind, had begun to shake.

The water continued to rise reaching the wheels of Tommy's new red pick-up and Matt's white explorer parked on the concrete parking area next to the house. We had taken Ann's 1995 red Crown Victoria to what we thought would be high ground at St. Augustine Seminary and drove my 1995 green Crown Vic to our daughter Cindy's yard which was about 30 yards away and on higher ground. Later I took lines off my 21 ft. Pro-Line boat and tied the boat to trees and also tied a line from our home to a tree in Cindy's yard to serve as a safety line from our house to hers in the event we had to evacuate we could get to the green Crown Vic and escape.

It wasn't long before the water had risen to the doors of the house but we had already begun to duct tape the doors to keep the water out. We taped about 3 feet up recalling that Camille had only risen about 1½ ft. on the outside of the house. When the water reached around the 2 ft. level outside I began to think, this should be about it. Certainly it should soon stop rising. I heard Tommy call and point to the terrazzo floor. Water was beginning to squirt up through the terrazzo joints and spread across the floor of the living room. The four of us began to use large sponges and towels to soak up the water and fill buckets. We opened the window to the carport outside the kitchen and began emptying the buckets outside. Then the tape on the doors began to leak and the water on the floors began to deepen. We gave up on sponging and began to bail in earnest with the buckets as the water deepened to 6 inches or more. At this point my mind began to admit that the situation was becoming critical and though what I recall is a little sketchy, I remember Bish and Matt crawling out the window to the carport to receive the buckets of water we were bailing.

At some point during this time I recall Matt and I going outside to where the boat was tied to get life jackets. The water now was beginning to run like a river past the house and westerly toward Second Street and the marsh. The wind seemed like a fist hitting us in extreme tornado-like gusts. I only found four jackets and a throwable cushion and until this day I don't know what happened to the others; I am sure I had more.

It was all Matt and I could do to get back to the house against the wind and water. At one point I found the safety line I had tied to Cindy's house and used it to get back to ours. Matt proved to be more able to cope as we re-entered the house and distributed the jackets. Afterwards, I recalled Matt asking if there were any more life jackets and I said there weren't. I remember him looking a little crestfallen and realized later that he and Bish had done without so that Toppy, Tommy, Ann and I would each have one.

Once back in the house, Tommy suddenly called me. I looked toward him at the front door. The tape was coming off the door and water was squirting through like a hose. Then at that moment the whole door was torn off its hinges and fell into the living room and water came gushing in. In no time furniture began floating around and the water was knee deep.

I yelled at everyone to follow me to our neighbor's house next door which was a good bit higher than ours. We opened the kitchen door and began wading to the Nordman's house. I held Ann's hand as all of us stumbled through the increasingly fast moving water. Toppy and Tommy, Bish and Matt followed carrying the dogs. If I remember correctly, Toppy was carrying Odie, a small dachshund, and Bish was carrying Peanut (they were very close friends.) I can't recall who had Dumplin, probably Tommy.

At times I am not certain necessarily of the sequence in which things occurred. I do remember now that at some point I had asked Bish to get extra buckets out of the garage which was separate from and behind the house and when he returned he said the garage doors were gone. The building was shaking so much from the wind he was afraid to enter. Later, I can recall him saying the garage itself was gone. After the hurricane we found that a huge oak next to the garage had fallen on it.

We finally reached the rear of the house next door and climbed the steps to the back porch. The wind was increasing to howling velocity and the water was getting deeper. Being on the windward side of the house we were being pummeled by the unbelievable power of the wind and decided to move into the house but the door was locked. Bish broke a small glass panel and was able to reach in and unlock the door. I recall that I had grabbed a blue and white cooler and hung on to it in the event we needed it for floatation.

We moved through the house to the front door hoping to make a stand on the downwind front porch. When we reached the front door we found that door was also locked. Bish and Matt removed a small window air conditioner, raised the window and one by one we all crawled through to the front porch. By now the water was considerably deeper and waves were beginning to form. I remember closely watching the porch railing and saw that the water was still rising. Now all we could do was hope that it would soon stop. But it didn't.

The next few moments are a little blurred in my mind. But I seem to recall seeing and feeling the wall of the porch begin to shake and collapse toward us and suddenly we were all in the water being swept away. I remember holding on to Ann and both of us being carried toward some crepe myrtle trees. We reached out and grabbed on. I don't know why we did this; it just seemed what we had to do.

I noticed that Tommy and Toppy had also grabbed on to a crepe myrtle about 15 feet upstream and upwind from us. Toppy was still holding on to Odie, the little dachshund. Suddenly, I saw Toppy lose her grip by Tommy and was swept away to another tree about 10 feet from Ann and me. She was crying and saying she thought she had broken her arm. What happened next is not too clear but I remember her trying to get to me but could not manage well against the current. I think I told Ann to hold on tight while I tried to reach Toppy. We met about half way and about the time I reached for her she lost Odie and began crying in earnest. Apparently we had gotten back close to Ann because later Ann recalled Toppy losing Odie and that she had reached out and had almost grabbed the puppy's tail.

I lost my grip on Toppy and she was swept back to the tree where she had been, still crying. I looked around and saw that Tommy was still holding on to the tree where he and Toppy had originally been. When he saw Toppy was in trouble he swam to her. I recall seeing the two of them together being carried away by the current.

By now I could no longer touch bottom and would guess the water depth to have been about 8 feet. Now, huge waves filled with debris kept rolling over us and each time I thought we were going to be torn loose from the trees. It was about then that one of them dragged my pants down to my knees and I tried in vain to reach down and pull them up with one hand while trying to keep a grip on the tree and Ann at the same time. The next wave powered over us and I had to use both hands to hold on and felt pants and under shorts slide down my legs and then they were gone and at the same time I felt my watch also slip off.

During this time I can recall seeing parts of houses, roofs, refrigerators and all sorts of furniture and floating household items swiftly floating by us along with an unbelievable amount of lumber and other debris. The sound of the wind was now deafening, like that of a train, and numerous items including sheets of plywood and tree limbs were flying through the air and I was glad we had the crepe myrtle tree between us and the windborne debris.

It was about then that there was a sudden and very noticeable change of the wind from the southeast to the southwest. I considered this a good sign. The wind was hauling westerly and would eventually go west then northerly which would drive the water back out into the Gulf.

It is difficult to recall how long we continued to hold on to the crepe myrtle but with each wave it became more difficult. I realized that we needed to let go rather than fight waves and debris. I yelled to Ann that we should let go but she seemed determined to hang on. She looked so small and fragile. I was amazed by the tenacity with which she continued to hold. Watching her frightened, yet brave, wet little face I realized just how much she meant to me and resolved that I would not lose her. Finally, she either let go or I half pulled her loose so we could remain together.

Once we let go we were swiftly carried away, literally enclosed by the wreckage of what was once the homes and businesses of Bay St. Louis, and possibly other towns to the East across the bay such as Henderson Point and Pass Christian. We were grasping at pieces of furniture for flotation, though our life jackets were really our life savers. Later, Ann said she had seen our beautiful hatch cover coffee table float by us. Earlier, while still at our house, we had watched a pelican float by occasionally thrusting his big beak into the water for a snack. A short time later, a beautiful golden cocker spaniel passed by comfortably sitting on a piece of floating furniture and seemed to be enjoying his sight-seeing voyage.

We were still moving at a good rate when Ann complained that something around her legs was pulling her down. I went under and ran my hands down her legs and felt what appeared to be T.V. antenna wire and was able to free it from her legs. When I next looked up I saw we were being swept toward the telephone and power lines which were level with the surface of the water in front of us—that meant that we had to be in at least twenty or more feet of water—that was scary. As we arrived at the power lines I pushed Ann under and then swam under myself.

I looked downstream and saw what appeared to be a "log jam" of debris and we were being carried rapidly toward it. When we reached it we were jammed against it and all the wreckage behind us arrived and began to crush us into the jam. I began to shove and push the debris away from us but it kept coming and the thought occurred to me that we could be seriously injured and if the jam did break up we would be carried into and over the marsh and eventually into the bay, the sound and possibly into the Gulf.

As the debris began to thicken and press against us I looked to the left and saw a small oak (later we would realize it was the top of a large oak.) I told Ann to swim for the oak and we both struggled against the current and floating objects and finally reached the limbs of the tree. We managed to climb onto the tree freeing ourselves from the crowding debris and slightly above the surface of the rapidly flowing water. Here, for the first time we were actually able to rest, and by comparison to the preceding hours, were reasonably comfortable. We found we could sit on one limb which was about a foot under water and hold on to a limb which was about two to three feet above.

We remained in the oak for awhile and looking upstream I saw the telephone pole (whose wires we had swum under) about twenty feet away. The lines were barely a foot or so above the water. I estimated that the water beneath us had to be twenty to twenty-five feet deep, possibly deeper. For some time now Ann had found great difficulty in breathing and I knew she had probably swallowed water as I had. It was muddy and very salty and I was afraid this would probably have some ill effects later. While in the tree we saw Toppy and Tommy not far from us. Toppy was wearing my bright green foul weather jacket. They had apparently found refuge on some floating object and appeared to be mostly out of the water. The wind, rain and occasional thunder was so loud that we could not communicate with them.

The water now, though still moving rapidly, was without the huge waves we had encountered earlier. As we rested I figured that in this water depth it would be quite some time before we could leave the tree and walk on firm ground and that we might have to spend the night in the tree. Ann said she didn't think she could handle that. My heart went out to her as I held her in the crook of my arm to allow her to be more comfortable. Her eyes would close occasionally and this frightened me, I didn't know whether it was fatigue or she was losing consciousness. I would ask rather loudly "Are you okay?" and she would open her eyes and say yes but that she was having trouble breathing. She had always been rather short-winded and I supposed that could be the problem. She had just been through an experience that would exhaust anyone.

While hanging onto the oak tree I had looked back generally where we had come from and noticed two motor boats floating about 40 yards from us. I thought that if I could swim to one of them I could pull it back to Ann and we could climb aboard and be a lot more comfortable and safe and not fear having to spend the night in the tree. I told Ann that I was going to get one of the boats and for her to stay where she was until I returned.

I let go of the tree and started swimming to the boats. After swimming a few strokes I realized that I was moving toward them at a pretty good clip. I had not noted that the direction of the current had changed 180 degrees and was now moving rapidly in the other direction. I was now being carried very rapidly toward the two boats. As I neared them I recognized that the second boat was mine! I decided to swim to my boat. The water was now moving so fast that I almost missed the boat but was able to grab the stern and the ladder. I climbed aboard and as I looked at all the trees and limbs around I realized that I certainly could not risk starting the motor, and more troubling, there was no way that I would be able to pull the boat back to Ann. Now I realized the terrible mistake I had made. I had left my wife in a weakened condition, precariously hanging from a tree in 25 feet of water and looking at the current roaring by from the direction in which I had to swim to get back to her I realized that I may not be able to get back to her! For the first time since this had all started I was thoroughly frightened.

I climbed out of the boat and into the fast moving water. I looked and tried to determine the direction I needed to go to get back to her. It all looked very confusing and I had become disoriented but I knew approximately where I needed to go and it was upstream. I tried to swim back but made no progress at all. Panic really gripped me then. What was happening to Ann? God, I wished I had not left her … and speaking of God, though I am not a deeply religious person, I looked up and said out loud "I need a little help down here, Lord, please help me get back to my wife!" I made a promise then if this wish was granted and I intend to keep it.

I had managed to swim laterally to a large oak and held on as the swift current tried to pull me away from it. I looked to my right and saw a green building which I could not identify but it appeared to be on high ground with a hose laying on the ground at its base and directly in front of me about 30 feet upstream toward the green house was a large bush. If I could get to that bush I might be able to walk or swim to the house and work my way upstream to where I thought Ann was.

I managed to hold on to the tree and found lines attached to it. One was very tight and another was tied to the tree but was loose. I didn't realize this at the time, maybe some of the salt water had gotten to my brain, but the green house that appeared to be on the ground was the apartment next to ours and was on 10 foot pilings and the hose that I thought might be on the ground was actually floating.

Looking upstream at the large bush between me and the apartment, I realized it was the huge camellia in our yard about half way between our house and the green apartment. The oak tree I was holding onto was the large oak by our front door. The line that was tight was tied to my boat and the one that was loose had been tied to our front porch. I was really disoriented.

I tried several times to swim to the large bush and even though my toes were able to barely touch bottom I could make no headway. The current was too strong. About then I realized that the life jacket I was wearing (even though it was a child size) was causing too much resistance to the water. I thought about taking it off and wondered if that was a good idea. So far it had helped save our lives. I don't believe either of us could have survived without them.

While still holding onto the large oak, I pulled up the loose line until I had the end of it in my hands. Carefully holding the line between my teeth I took off my jacket and tied it to the end of the line and released it. It moved rapidly down steam, submerged briefly then rose to the surface and stopped. Now if I tried to swim to the large bush and lost my balance and was swept back with the current I could try to catch the tree first and if I missed the tree I could grab the life jacket and stop from being carried away by the current. I was standing with my back pressed against the tree facing the oncoming water and if I happened to move a little too far left or right the rushing water would try to pull me loose.

Realizing that I could not swim directly against the current I looked to my left and saw a line of bushes and small trees which ran in the direction I wanted to go. I let go of the large oak and began to furiously swim across the current and though I was carried farther downstream I was able to reach the bushes and trees. I then began grabbing limbs and vines pulling myself in the direction of the apartment. I finally reached it and saw then that it was on pilings with the water almost level with the floor of the building. Later I found out that I had swum over my green Crown Vic which had been swept from Cindy's yard and had been crushed and lodged against the pilings.

I swam and pulled myself from piling to piling and then to more bushes and tree limbs. As I progressed I intermittently cried out for Ann and when I received no answer I became more and more despondent and directed more prayers above.

I suddenly noticed a couple of telephone poles and remembered that shortly after Ann and I had climbed onto the oak we had watched one of the poles and its hardware to see if the water was falling. I spotted the one I thought it might be and began swimming toward it. I now found it easier to swim. The current had appreciably slowed down and the next time I called out for Ann she answered! That was the happiest moment of my life. We continued to call to each other until I finally found her.

I had left her sitting on a limb that was about a foot under water while she held on to another about 2 feet above her head. Now the limb she was sitting on was about three feet above the water. The water was almost calm now but still receding at a fairly rapid rate. Ann expressed a concern about the falling water and was afraid of being stranded well up the large tree and not being able to get down. She wanted down now and pointed to a couple of upside down sunfish lashed to a trailer and wanted me to help her get to them or bring them to her.

I had just begun to swim toward the sunfish when I heard voices and when I looked in that direction what I saw was a welcome as well as humorous sight. Paddling toward us on another sunfish were Bishop and Matt, with the two dogs, Peanut and Dumplin. It appeared they were using pieces of lumber as paddles and as they approached Bish cried out "Hi, Pop." What a pleasant, warm feeling surged through me. Until then we did not know whether they were alive or not. They paddled under the tree and managed to ease Ann from the oak limb down to the sunfish without the boat turning over, which as I think about it now was somewhat of a remarkable feat.

Bish then turned and looked at me and said, "Okay, Dad, your turn. Come aboard." I considered this for a moment, realizing that all I had on in the way of clothes was my shirt. Though modesty probably should not have been a concern when lives were at stake, I looked up at Bish and said, "Uh … I've got a problem." Ann explained and Bish and Matt could hardly control their laughter. "Well, hang on while we head to the green apartment." I did not know, at the time, but the boys had already made contact with Toppy and Tommy and planned to rescue them also.

Bish and Matt paddled and I swam and pushed from the stern. We made it to the apartment and the boat slid over the fence between our yards. I let go of the stern and very carefully managed to swim and crawl over the fence toward the steps leading upstairs. Before emerging from the water, however, I took off my long sleeved shirt and managed to tie it around my waist like a sarong.

Ann and I and the two dogs climbed the stairs while Bish and Matt paddled back to pick up Toppy and Tommy. Once inside and out of the wind I began to search for more adequate clothing. The cottage had been gutted by the water and waves and was a mess but we did manage to find some dry T-shirts on a high shelf and a relatively dry blanket to wrap around me.

It wasn't long before the boys returned with Toppy and Tommy and we were all huddled into the living room, dogs and all. It was then that we began to be aware of our wounds. Ann's arms and legs were severely scratched and torn. Toppy was nursing what appeared to be a broken or fractured arm. Tommy had a terrible, open abrasion on his right arm. And Matt pointed out that my right foot was bleeding. I looked down and was really surprised to see that it was. We all agreed that we should seek medical attention as soon as possible. Dry clean clothing would also be a big help.

The water around us was rapidly receding and from the porch I looked toward our home and saw green grass beginning to appear—but no home! What a frightening realization. It was hard to comprehend that everything Ann and I had accumulated over the past 53 years had been destroyed. The necessities of coping with the present thankfully diverted my thoughts.

Matt volunteered to try to make it to his home where he and our daughter, Tracey, lived to see if he could find dry clothing. I believe Bish went with him, and Peanut, who was closely enamored to Bish, would not be left behind, so the three of them left on their mission.

While Toppy, Tommy, Ann and I, along with Dumplin, waited for the boys and Peanut to return, we realized that Ann's and Tommy's wounds were quite serious and they really needed to see a doctor. After awhile the boys and Peanut returned with dry clothes and shoes. Matt had brought me a pair of his sandals and plaid pajama pants (thank goodness for the elastic waistline—Matt being slim and trim and I not). Matt and Tracey's home had been really messed up as apparently about three feet of water had surged through it. He had found clothing and shoes on some shelves that had been above water. We put on the dry clothes and sandals and decided to go to the hospital for our various wounds.

Here happenings are a little hazy. After Matt and Bish helped us stumble our way through mounds of debris and mud to highway 90, which was relatively clear, I believe they and Peanut went back to Matt's home or possibly to Walter Rausch's home where Walter and Malin Chamberlain were staying with their son, Gilly, and were to meet us at the hospital later. I believe they were looking for a place for us to stay and were also trying to contact our daughter, Cindy, and her husband, Larry, in Houston by cell phone. Communication with the world outside of Bay St. Louis was all but impossible. There were no "landlines" working and cell phones were having a more than difficult time.

Somehow, Toppy and Tommy had preceded Ann and me to the hospital. I remember Ann and I hitch-hiked on a school bus to Hancock Medical Center. We entered the hospital emergency room where nurses and doctors were already treating the wounded. We were advised by a nurse that the hospital had had 3 feet of water throughout and had no electricity or water but they would do what they could to help us. I began to realize then the magnitude of the surge that had slammed into Bay St. Louis and Waveland.

Ann had her arms cleansed with saline and I believe treated with a topical anesthetic/antibiotic. There were no antibiotics by injection available but we did both receive tetanus shots. What a feeling of relief these nurses and doctors imparted to us. Wonderful people, most with their own problems resulting from Katrina but were there dedicating themselves to others. Both the doctors and nurses were very concerned about Ann's wounds and gave her a lot of attention.

From the emergency room we were guided to the cafeteria and were able to get a bite to eat and something to drink. We finally met up with Toppy and Tommy. Both were treated as well as possible. They were concerned about Toppy's and Tommy's arms and suggested that they go to Stennis Space Center whose facilities were operative.

We left the hospital and met Bish and Matt outside and started walking back toward Walter Rausch's home where Bish and Matt had arranged for all of us to stay. A police van picked us up and drove us in a roundabout way (I think they were from out of town and didn't really know their way around too well) to Second Street and from there we walked to Hickory Lane and on to Walter Rausch's home where we were warmly greeted by the Chamberlains and Walter Rausch, a 91 year old perfect gentleman and host. His home had been invaded by about 2 feet of water and a thick layer of black mud.

We were offered freshly cut oranges and lemonade to drink. Ann was not feeling well and ate very little. We were all dead tired, of course, and really needed rest. We were led by Malin and her flashlight to a bedroom with twin beds where we were to sleep and were shown where the bathroom was and the procedure to use the facilities since there was no running water anywhere. The floor was carpeted and with the layer of mud it was a very slippery proposition to walk without falling. Back in the bedroom we wasted little time trying to go to sleep. Their house was still boarded up tight with no circulation, no air conditioning, of course, and sweat just rolled down my face and body and I couldn't see how I could get to sleep, but we did after carefully removing our shoes and trying not to get too much mud on the bed.

Morning came and I'm embarrassed to say the events of the next day are a little muddled in my mind. I do recall that we had tied Peanut to a tree the night before but being a house dog she wanted to be inside with us and barked steadily in protest of being tied up outside. I believe it was Bish who took her down the street and tied her up at Matt and Tracey's home with water and some food where she spent the night, probably barked herself to sleep but we couldn't hear her.

Sally and her daughters, Sarah and Brittany, arrived for a visit. Their home on Ulman Avenue (where we had assured her there would be no water) had 3 feet of the surge pass through and had left it a mess. Sally and the girls had evacuated to a shelter.

During the day Bish and Matt spent most of their time trying to contact the outside world, specifically, Cindy and Larry in Houston. At some point Bish had managed to get through in short bursts of communication but finally got the word to Larry: "Our situation is desperate!" and based on that one sentence Larry and Cindy begin to move quickly gathering friends, vehicles and supplies for Bay St. Louis. We were really not aware of the "convoy" heading for us. I think that one contact by Bish and his brief message was all we knew.

I thought that perhaps we might see Woody, another and oldest of our sons who was living in a trailer at the Bible Baptist Church North of I-10 and was apparently not aware of the immensity of destruction along the coast but was very busy taking care of a substantial number of church members who had severe wind damage to their homes.

We had left a sign at the slab that was once our home advising that we were at Tracey and Matt's house so I set up camp so to speak waiting for Woody or whoever might come to our assistance. The day wore on. Toppy and Tommy had been so anxious about the condition of their new home which was at the end of Blue Meadow road, right on the Jourdan River, that Matt and Bish set out on bicycles to ride there and find out.

Their home was approximately 4 to 5 miles from where we were staying. Bish ended up with a bike that was no longer functional and had to return. Matt continued, mud and all, sometimes having to carry his bike across deep mud or piles of debris or fallen trees, until he finally reached their home. It was standing but badly damaged. Their home I believe was about 10 ft. above sea level and the surge had been about 6 ft above their floor which had partially collapsed, with Toppy's beautiful baby grand piano trying to fall through.

I mention the piano but of course both she and Tommy lost many of their prized possessions, as did Sally, Matt and Tracey and thousands of other families along the coast and well inland.

The day passed and as the evening arrived we were all sitting in the living room at Walter Rausch's home. Someone had procured some food from somewhere and when we had finished our community dinner together, Walter Chamberlain produced a bottle of red wine which was evenly distributed in paper cups. We had lit a candle on a coffee table and were gathered around chatting by the dim but friendly light of the candle. There was Walter Rausch, still the perfect host and gentleman, unaffected by the mud and heat and darkness. We were all his invited guests and he the perfect host. Though hard of hearing, whenever he could participate, he was an excellent conversationalist. Then there were the rest of us: Walter, Malin, Gilly, Bish, Matt, Ann and me.

Walter R. suddenly said, "Let's have some entertainment. Walter, get your banjo and play for us. You too, Gilly, get your guitar and let's have some music.

I'm sorry to admit this, but I was not really enthusiastic about this. I was tired and depressed about our circumstances and Walter R's suggestion just didn't fit my mood. Well, as I look back now, I realize that Walter R. recognized this in most of us there and he knew what the cure was.

Walter C. and Gilly left the room and returned with their instruments. They both spent a few seconds tuning up. And even with the non-melodic strokes of the strings in tuning my spirits began to lift. Then Walter C. began to play as only Walter can. He has played professionally for years in New Orleans, along the Gulf Coast and at many Bay-Waveland Yacht Club functions. The whole atmosphere of the room changed as the wonderful sound of the banjo permeated the hearts of all of us. He selected many favorites and at some point Gilly began to accompany him in a duet and the sound was absolutely wonderful. Whatever depressing thoughts had occupied my mind disappeared.

Walter C. stopped for a moment and looked at Gilly who began to improvise a song of "Katrina", composing the words as he played and it was great. I do hope he kept the words. I would like to hear them again someday. And I would certainly like to hear more of the father and son duets again. As Gilly finished his "Song of Katrina" there was a short period of silence as we all dwelled over the pleasure their music had provided.

The silence ended abruptly as the older Walter suddenly said, "I cannot play an instrument, but I can recite." I had no idea what he was talking about but I saw him sit up erect in his chair and for a moment seemed to stare at an object somewhere beyond the room.

"Gunga Din!" he said, his voice enunciating the words with the absolute clarity of a true Englishman. He then recited the entire poem by Rudyard Kipling verbatim. His inflections were perfect and his countenance shone the enthusiasm he felt about Gunga Din. He continued the poem with heartfelt emotion to its end: "Though I've belted you and flayed you, by the living God that made you, you're a better man than I am, Gunga Din."

As the poem ended, we gave him a standing ovation. And if Walter had been center stage anywhere in the world he would have brought down the house with applause. I will never forget that evening as long as I live and I will never think of Gunga Din again without thinking of Walter Rausch.

We were subsequently rescued by our son-in-law, Larry Cady, and his convoy of very special friends from Houston, Brad and John. Subsequently, and in short order, we were driven to Houston by Matt in Brad's Suburban to become guests of Larry and Cindy. Here Ann and I recovered physically and mentally for about a month and eventually moved to our son, Dennis's home in Woolmarket, Mississippi, where he and his wife Debbie and their children, Tim, Rachel, Melanie and Elizabeth and their wonderful yellow lab, Angel, made us feel loved and at home while we looked forward to our new home in Diamondhead, Mississippi and a new life together.

978-0-595-41780-3
0-595-41780-9